FROM A BESTSELLING AUTHOR OF THE 39 CLUES SERIES

JUDE WATSON

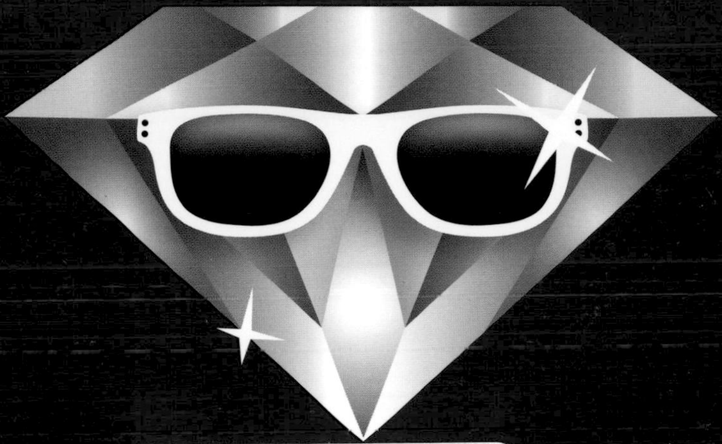

"OOT hits the jackpot."
—RICK RIORDAN
#1 *New York Times* bestselling author

LOOT

HOW TO STEAL A FORTUNE

SCHOLASTIC

ISBN 978-0-545-46803-9
50699
EAN
9 780545 468039

EVERYBODY LOVES **LOOT**!

"So many things I love about this book: Cursed jewels, a dangerous prophecy, a crash course in the history of thievery, acrobatics and grift. . . . It's the perfect summer read for kids."

— Rick Riordan, #1 *New York Times* bestselling author of the Percy Jackson series

"**LOOT** is one of those books that you'll want to devour in one sitting. Full of twists and turns and thrills aplenty."

— James Dashner, #1 *New York Times* bestselling author of *The Maze Runner*

"**LOOT** is pure delight — a super-smart, funny, and exciting ride."

— Rebecca Stead, *New York Times* bestselling author and Newbery Medalist for *When You Reach Me*

"A nonstop thrill ride of cons, schemes, and near-misses, with more twists than a pretzel factory."

— Gordon Korman, #1 *New York Times* bestselling author of *Swindle*

"An edge-of-your seat mystery that manages to be thrilling, funny, nail-biting, and full of real characters readers will care about. I loved it."

— Peter Lerangis, *New York Times* bestselling author of the Seven Wonders series

"**LOOT** is one of my favorite reads in a very long time!"

— Jennifer A. Nielsen, *New York Times* bestselling author of *The False Prince*

"Bursting with adventure, humor, and heart, **LOOT** is an unputdownable treat. Just make sure to hide it somewhere genius when you're done, so no one tries to steal it."

— Sarah Mlynowski, *New York Times* bestselling author of the Whatever After series

"A page-turner full of action and heart. This is *Ocean's Eleven* for the middle grade reader."

— Kirby Larson, Newbery Honor author of *Hattie Big Sky*

"**LOOT** breezes along in Jude Watson's trademark smart, snappy style, a sophisticated caper with a charming and unforgettable cast of characters."

— Natalie Standiford, author of *The Secret Tree*

"**LOOT** . . . will keep kids flipping pages long after lights out."

— Rachel Vail, author of *Unfriended*

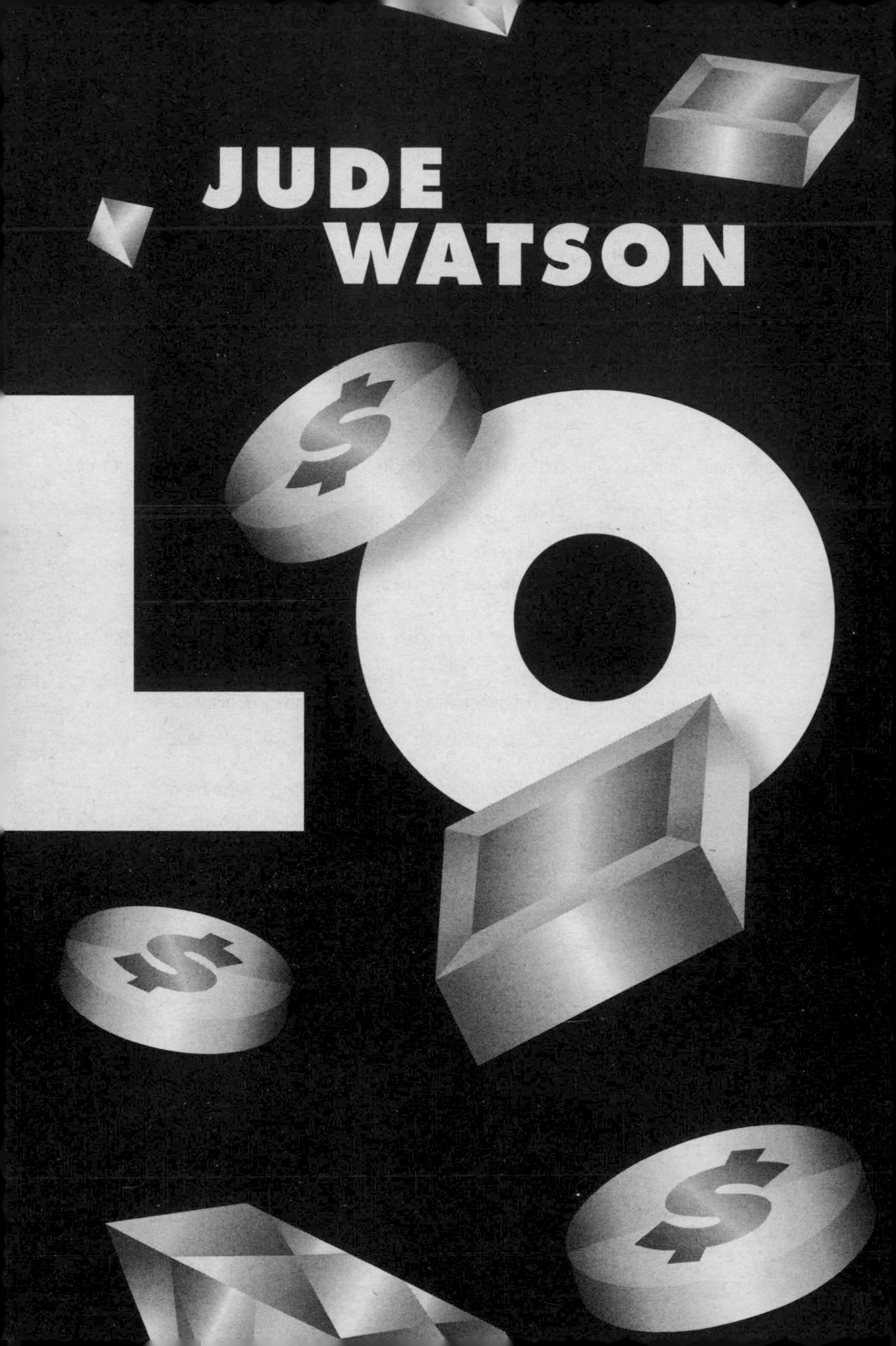
JUDE
WATSON

OT

HOW TO STEAL A FORTUNE

SCHOLASTIC INC.

This book was originally published in hardcover by Scholastic Press in 2014.

ISBN 978-0-545-46803-9

12 11 10 9 8 7 6 5 4 3 2 1   15 16 17 18 19 20/0

Printed in the U.S.A. 40
First printing 2015

The text type was set in Adobe Garamond Pro.
Book design by Nina Goffi

TO BAD CHILDREN EVERYWHERE

"Behind every great fortune there is a crime."

— Honoré de Balzac

BEFORE
FROZEN MOONLIGHT

No thief likes a full moon. Like mushrooms and owls, they do their best work in the dark.

There it is, a fat, satisfied moon, bright and silvery white, tracing a line on the dark lake that leads right to three thieves, who have paused to examine the loot.

It has been the perfect heist. In and out, a hot knife through sweet butter. Months of planning, practice runs, disagreements that ballooned into fights. Two of the thieves are barely speaking to the third.

In the end, it didn't matter.

In the end, they got the goods.

A priceless emerald brooch owned by Catherine the Great.

The Crack in the Sky, the world's most famous turquoise.

The sixty-carat Makepeace Diamond, said to be the most brilliant gem in the history of the world.

The stones are all notorious. Cursed. Rumored to have caused more deaths, bankruptcies, suicides, and indigestion than any moldering mummy could even hope to inspire.

The owner of all these jewels? Carlotta Grimstone, one of the richest women on the planet. Early on in her career as a socialite, she found herself competing with prettier, sillier girls for attention. She liked getting her picture in the paper. So, with Daddy's permission, she decided to make a name for herself by collecting all of the world's cursed stones. She even dreamed up a nickname and hired a publicist to drop it to any media outlet that would listen and print it. But "Fate's Temptress" never stuck.

Thieves don't believe in curses. How can something worth so much be cursed? It's a ticket to a sweet life. The only people who say money can't buy happiness are the poor suckers shining a billionaire's shoes.

The stones wink at them from a flat rock, catching the moonlight.

Hello, sweet life, they are all thinking.

But even a perfect heist has its pitfalls.

The third thief has violated their agreement. He has snatched up a pretty necklace for his girlfriend. It's a bauble, not nearly worth what the other stones are. He wants to keep it.

There are objections. They don't know what these seven moonstones in the necklace are worth, but they look unusually fine. Since he violated the terms of the heist, why should he get the spoils?

Fine, the third thief says, snatching up the necklace and twirling it around his finger in an arc. *Then fence it with the others. Sell it to another crook for less than it's worth, if it makes you happy.*

The clasp breaks, the gold links falling away, and the moonstones seem to hover in the air — how is *that* possible? — before falling onto the rocky beach.

The stones form a perfect circle. It's as though drops of moonlight have frozen on the ground. They glow with a light that is not quite blue, not quite white, not quite silver.

It is the most beautiful sight the three thieves have ever seen.

So beautiful that they cannot move. They can't look away.

Then there comes a shock to their bodies, so electric it takes their breath. Dread runs through them like ice through rock. They might shatter from it.

The third thief sees himself captured. *You will be caught tonight and made to pay.*

The second thief receives a death sentence. *Death by water, before the moon is set.*

The first thief sees the worst vision of all. *Before the passage of thirteen years, the two birthed together will die together.*

The sound of a helicopter wakes them up out of what feels like a trance.

The searchlight sweeps the water and the path of light hits the beach. It lands on the third thief.

He snarls the curses that people who have been unlucky enough to find themselves caught use. He blames the other two. *Betrayed!*

With quicker reflexes, the other two have dived behind a boulder, flattened against it, pressing themselves into shadow. The third thief — the angry one — is closest to the emerald brooch and the Crack in the Sky. The Makepeace Diamond rolls away from his fingers. He grabs the other two gems and runs full tilt toward any shadow he can find. The searchlight follows him.

The circle of moonstones is just inches away from the two thieves. Pressed against the shadow, one thief dares to reach out and scoop up the stones. The two dash through the boulders toward the line of trees.

They have practiced this route many times, and they know it well. Through the woods, around the lake, to the cliff. They scramble up the cliff quickly, knowing each handhold. Vaulting over the top, they race to the cover of the pines. They slip into the entrance to the cave.

Even in early summer, the cave glitters with ice. The mist cools their skin.

They know each other so well. They don't need to exchange a word. One glance does it.

Coincidence. It won't happen to us. No such thing as prophecies.

How can you be so sure?

Because I'm rational.

According to who? You're standing in an ice cave with a bag of moonstones and the police are after you. That's rational?

It's amazing what you can do with your eyes.

The fall of water against the cave wall is like a mirror reflecting darkness. They drop on their hands and knees and half-crawl, half-slither through a crack in the wall.

They inch out slowly to the open air. They are high above the lake now. The thunder of the waterfall surprises them, so much more powerful than they'd seen before. The stones under their feet are slick and glitter with ice.

The second thief turns, smiles, is ready to say something. Slips on the slick, wet rock.

This is not part of the plan.

The thief goes over backward, swept into the torrent.

The first thief's cry is an anguished howl.

1

NOW

POCKETFUL OF STONES

Never trust a guy who says, "Trust me."
Never give your real name to a cop.
Never let someone steal your getaway car.

It was that last piece of his father's advice that March McQuin found himself contemplating at three in the morning on a picturesque bridge over a dark canal in Amsterdam. Only it wasn't a getaway *car*, it was a getaway bike, and someone had pinched it.

Just about the worst thing you can do to a thief is steal his stuff. March was especially indignant. He'd actually *paid for* the bike!

He checked the time on his cell. He felt the pressure in his drumming pulse, but he wasn't about to panic. He just had to steal a bike. In about seven minutes, his old man, world-famous cat burglar Alfred McQuin, was going to have a fistful of diamonds and be looking for an exit.

That would be March.

Mist curled along the surface of the canal. All the good citizens of Amsterdam were snoring underneath their eiderdowns. The weeping edges of a yellow moon dissolved and re-formed on dark water as the flow of the tide moved through. March intently scanned the row of bicycles chained to the railing, searching for his target.

Timing is everything, bud. The difference between a million bucks and twenty-five-to-life can come down to thirty seconds.

The red one with the basket and the combination lock called to March: *Steal me!*

Battered fenders, but the chain was oiled and the tires were good.

There were roughly sixty-four thousand different number sequences possible in one combination lock. He could find the correct one in a minute flat. All it took was the right touch. March felt for the slight drag as the chamber hit the number. Again. Got it. Then counterclockwise. Clockwise again. The lock swung open.

He took the time to let out a long, shaky breath. If he messed up, Alfie would forgive him, but he'd never forgive himself.

He threw his brown-paper sack in the basket. The cover story had been decided on a week ago. If he got stopped by a cop, he was bringing his night watchman father his breakfast. There was *bruine boterham met kaas* — brown bread and cheese — and an apple in the sack.

Remember, the right prop can save a shaky cover story.

March flew over the bridge, legs pumping hard. He'd been over the route many times. He had walked it with Alfie, both of them munching on herring sandwiches, looking like what Alfie called ham-and-eggers, the normal American tourists their fake passports claimed they were: Dan Sherwood, from Syosset, Long Island, and his son Dan Jr. Then he'd ridden it a half-dozen times, with Alfie timing him. They'd gone over every detail, and nothing could go wrong.

Even though Alfie always said: *If you think nothing can go wrong, you'd better think again.*

He flew down the last street and turned the corner. The grand hotel rose up from the canal like a tanker about to sail to the North Sea. He cut the bike toward the rear courtyard, bumped over the cobblestones to the loading dock, and skidded to a stop, only a minute late. Any second his pop should be shimmying down the drainpipe and tossing him the jewels.

Trying to slow the urgent racing of his heart, he scanned the façade of the hotel.

No Pop.

When trying to spot Alfred McQuin, it was always smart to check the roof.

March craned his neck and looked up. Alfie was just a dark shadow moving along the dormers, high above the cobblestone courtyard.

The first faint alarm began to ding inside him. There was improvisation in even the tightest plan, but something must have gone wrong. Unless his timing was off. He checked his cell again.

March glanced back up, and this time Alfie was looking down at him.

They had a secret signal when they bumped into each other accidentally in public and Alfie didn't want March to acknowledge him. He would smooth his left eyebrow.

It meant, *I'm working, get out of here.*

But why now? Had something gone wrong? Alfie's hand moved, and he tossed something off the roof. It seemed to catch the moonlight, then hover and spin, something bright and bluish white and as small as a star.

Before he had time to think, March ran toward it. It seemed to fall in slow motion, and he felt as though he had all the time in the world to catch it. He opened the paper bag, and it fell inside with the slightest little ping.

March looked inside to see what it was. It was that smallest space of a moment, that beat of a heart, that counted. Because the next time he looked up, his father was falling.

2

FLOATING/FALLING

Alfie fell backward through the air, face to the night sky, as though he had said to himself, *The heck with climbing down. Think I'll just float.*

The dropping seemed to take forever.

March felt his cry explode from his gut, but it stayed inside. All his life he'd been trained not to express emotion in public unless it was manufactured, part of a plan.

The sound of the landing was like no sound March had ever heard. It seemed like a sound a watermelon would make, or a plastic jug of water. Not a person.

March ran. The last few inches he slid on his knees against the stones. Stone against bone.

"Pop . . ."

Alfie seemed strangely unbruised, filling March with hope. Then he noticed the blood pooling behind his father's head.

Alfie's hand came up, fingers fluttering like a sputtering candle. March reached for that hand to still those fingers. He had never seen his father with shaking hands. Jewel thieves don't have hands that tremble.

"March."

He swallowed against the fear that constricted his throat. "Pop, I —"

"Wait . . . a month."

"What?"

Alfie coughed, a terrible, awful sound, thick and bubbling. "Promise. A month!"

"Promise, but —"

"Then find jewels." Each word came out as a small puff of air. "Stick. Rag."

With what seemed like enormous effort, his father touched March's cheek and his hair.

"Follow the falls to day . . ."

"Don't die," March pleaded. "Please don't die."

"No."

Blood frothed and came out of Alfie's mouth. His eyes were unfocused now, staring up at the moon.

March collapsed back on his heels. He didn't believe in this moment. He hung suspended in it, but it wasn't real. Surely he could change it. He could return to himself on the bridge, he could pedal faster, and then he'd have time to yell, "Don't slip!" or "Watch out!"

March heard a siren, that European *wee-oh, wee-oh* sound, and footsteps running and stopping behind him.

The moment was over, time had ticked on, and it took him to a place where his father was dead.

Behind him there were sudden fragments of sound and movement. A half circle of people talking in hushed voices — the doorman. A couple of kitchen workers.

The ambulance drew up. A police car squealed to a halt. The officials were here.

You see a uniform, you scram.

March stumbled away as the ambulance workers ran over. He kept backing up, his eyes on the medics. He watched them bend over the body, shine a light in Alfie's eyes, feel for a pulse, get out equipment. They cut away Alfie's jacket, and diamonds spilled out of his pockets.

The small crowd gasped. The police perked up.

March saw the instant the medics gave up. Two of them exchanged a glance and one shook his head. Their movements slowed, and one of them started to put equipment away. There was no need to hurry now. A terrible anguish filled his chest and pressed against his heart.

More talking in Dutch. The circle around Alfie was growing. A couple of hotel guests had heard the commotion and come out. Tomorrow it would be a story: how a man with diamonds in his pockets fell down from the sky.

One policeman squatted over the body. He said a name with great excitement.

Alfred McQuin.

And then someone in the circle, the guy in the white apron, the baker, trying to be helpful, was pointing, and March picked out a word he knew.

Jongen. Boy.

Waar is de jongen?

By the time someone pointed again, it was to air.

3

WHERE IS THE BOY

Boy alone on the street, 3:00 a.m., don't run, don't be seen, keep close to the buildings, keep your eyes open, move fast. Panic doesn't get you anything except arrested. If you get stopped, remember your cover story.

March had lost the map in his head. The route he'd memorized was gone. The streets suddenly looked all the same, with their narrow houses with sharply peaked roofs and tidily painted doors. Yellow, blue, red, black. There wasn't a straight line in Amsterdam; all the buildings seemed to tilt. It felt to March as though they would tumble down on him, a shower of bricks and window boxes full of tulips.

Waar is de jongen?

Where is the boy?

Nothing felt real except the pavement against the soles of his sneakers.

How hard it had been for his father to touch his cheek! How much strain on his face, how much determination. When the gesture had been done so casually so many times. A hand on his shoulder. A kiss on the top of his head. He'd never feel that again.

March saw the days ahead of him, so many days and years, when he wouldn't feel that hand.

March's knees gave way. He sat on the sidewalk. He knew he shouldn't. No doubt some stray insomniac would look outside his bedroom window, and his proper Dutch mind would want to get help for the boy collapsed in the middle of the sidewalk, holding his head with both hands.

Tears dripped through his fingers. He scrubbed them away. Shock made everything so sharp, and yet so far away.

The paper bag sat in his lap. In it was the cheese sandwich they were going to split for breakfast, back at the flat. March thought of the many things his father loved and would never eat again. *Pommes frites* and herring sandwiches and American potato chips and licorice. Things he said they'd do together: see a Yankees game, spend a month in New Zealand, go to a museum without playing the "what would you steal and how" game.

March tossed the bag aside, hating the sandwich because Alfie would never eat it.

The stone tumbled out, aglow in the moonlight.

It was the last thing his father had given him. Maybe it was worth something? Or else why had Alfie thrown it, knowing March would catch it, because his son had never let him down?

Just yesterday, he'd said it.

You've never let me down, March.

March gripped the stone hard. *Don't let him down, then. Keep moving.*

It took only a block before he knew he was being followed.

4

ME AND MY SHADOW

It wasn't as easy as footfalls behind him. No. Someone was following him, but someone was very, very good at it.

You couldn't be the son of a master thief if you didn't grow a sixth sense.

Panic shimmered through his body, tiny hammers hitting glass. He could shatter, he felt, in a moment, and he gulped air, trying to calm himself.

The guy waited to turn corners until March did. As March crossed a canal and started down the other side, he stayed as close as he could between the boats and the parked cars on the side of the canal.

With water to amplify the echoes, March heard the footsteps clearly. He walked faster. The pace behind him increased.

Police? He didn't think so.

He still didn't know where he was, but that didn't matter now. He had to lose whoever it was before he headed to the apartment. But *why* was someone following him? It didn't make sense. Unless he was imagining it.

He knew he wasn't.

Down one more block, around a corner, loop back, and cross the canal again. Still the footsteps followed. He turned a corner around an apartment building and stopped to peer around it.

Across the misty water, a figure strolled along the brick

pathway. March couldn't see a face underneath the black cap. Hands in pockets of a loose raincoat.

Just a person, out for a late-night walk? Coming home from a party?

The figure followed the curve of the canal and disappeared around a bend. March waited another minute, suddenly nervous about moving. Which direction should he head?

Then he heard the footsteps again, tapping along the brick pathway. This time his pursuer was on *his* side of the canal. Panic was now a frantic drumbeat inside him. He pushed off the building and sprinted down the side of the canal.

March dodged in between cars parked at the edge of the canal and slid into one of the boats tied up alongside. He edged under a tarp that had been tossed next to the cabin.

The footsteps continued toward him, down the side of the canal where he had just been.

Tap, tap, tap . . .

The person stopped near the boat.

He held his breath.

Long seconds passed. March's fingers shook as he held the tarp over his head.

All sound left the world. The lapping of the water against the hull of the boat, the faint sound of a tram rattling down a street blocks away, his own skittering pulse . . . He heard nothing now as he strained to hear something — a rustle of a coat, the tapping of the footsteps heading away.

Instead he heard, faintly, the sound of . . . whistling. A tune March didn't recognize, something eerie that caught on moonlight and curled along the mist. One long note, one short, then a simple melody.

The person stopped whistling abruptly. If March had moved, the person would have heard the rustle. Was that the reason for the abrupt stop . . . to trap him into revealing himself?

A quiet footfall, heading closer.

The person was standing right next to the boat. The whistling began again. Two long notes . . . Then the melody.

March raised the edge of the tarp a tiny fraction. The person was pulling on black leather gloves. Why? It wasn't cold.

No fingerprints. He jerked in terror, kicking something that clanged softly.

The whistling stopped.

A light turned on in the cabin below him. He felt, through the wood of the deck, two feet hitting the floor. Someone called out in Dutch, something angry. The door flew open and a man came out on deck, shirtless and barefoot. He tripped over the tarp and kicked it in frustration.

His bare foot met March's leg.

With a roar, he threw the tarp back.

March bolted. He had time to register the flash of anger and surprise on the burly man's face, creased with sleep. He felt rather than saw his pursuer standing still and watchful on the pavement. He jumped up on a deck chair, then onto the roof of the cabin, leaped onto the bow, then onto the stern of the next boat, scrambled up on the cabin, vaulted down into the open boat in front, and, with a combination of leap and stumble and scramble, his heart bursting, ran from boat to boat until he was able to leap up to the railing of the bridge, pull himself up and onto it, and look back.

The man on the boat stood bare chested and furious, shaking a fist and shouting in Dutch. A light came on in a house to his left.

The hem of a raincoat flapped as his pursuer hurried around a corner and disappeared.

5

WHAT NEXT

It took him three tries to lock the door of the apartment. He slid down until he was on the floor, back against the door, legs splayed out in front of him.

He tucked his hands in his armpits and ordered the caterwaul of panic to slow.

It didn't mean someone was following him, he told himself.

Someone could have been walking, strolling home. Who wouldn't have run like that when a man started yelling at a crazy kid who ran over boats to get away?

He had to stare down this terror.

He had to focus on what to do now.

Whether to hide or whether to run.

It wasn't like Alfie was the best father in the world. Not exactly a role model. There had been times over the years when he had pulled off a big job — two whole years living in the south of France, sweet! — but mostly he and March had bounced around Europe, with a couple of six-month stints in New York City and a very pleasant year in Spokane, Washington. March spent six months at a Swiss boarding school. They were both miserable. He still remembered the day he came out of class and saw Alfie leaning against a red convertible.

"Want to go for a spin?" he'd asked.

They'd driven to Spain.

So mostly March had been homeschooled, if you could call it that. His education was spotty. He knew the population of Istanbul and how to get around Reykjavík and the names of Beethoven's symphonies and could tell a Picasso from a Braque, but March couldn't multiply a fraction. He could calculate odds at a racetrack, though.

They were together, a team, and there were plenty more good times than bad.

March didn't know how to keep going without Alfie.

He remained on the floor, back against the door. He was used to being alone, but when alone has the promise of company at the end of it, it isn't quite as lonely. This was as lonesome as the moon. The deep kind of lonesome that held hands with fear.

All his life he'd felt as though something was missing. It would expand and contract inside him, like air inside a balloon. There were times he'd feel the space was so full that he'd turn to say something, and be surprised to find there was no one there.

Weird stuff.

As he got older he'd figured that the missing space was his mother. She'd died when he was two, so maybe some part of his brain remembered her.

But maybe all along he knew this feeling was coming for him.

This much empty filling him up.

The light was getting grayer outside. Soon the day would begin. The news would come on, the papers would hit the coffeehouses and cafés. People would open their laptops. The landlady on the first floor would turn on the radio.

Alfred McQuin, world-famous jewel thief, on Interpol's most wanted list, was dead. There would be a photograph, the most recent one they had, and the landlady would know that Alfie McQuin was Dan Sherwood in room 12, and she would call the police. She would say, "He has a son."

And then the knock at the door would come, and he'd be in the system. There would be paperwork and social workers and People Who Know Best. March would land back in the States, no doubt about that, because he had an American passport. Well. He had many passports, but only one real one, and that was American.

He had no relatives at all. Alfie's parents were dead, and he and March's mom had both been only children. Alfie thought she had family somewhere — Texas or Canada, he'd say, as if the two places were the same — but he'd never met them. So that meant foster care.

March knew how to navigate airports and train stations. How to pack light. How to move through a city without being noticed. How to order street food in Shanghai and steak au poivre in Paris. How to find a cheap apartment. He knew where to go to buy a fake passport in five European capitals and he knew how much it cost.

Things he didn't know how to do: Sit in a classroom. Obey authority. Follow rules.

6

WALKING-AWAY MONEY

Never look back, kid.

March gathered his nerve. He knew the drill; he'd watched Alfie do it a few times when they came a little too close to getting caught.

March went around the small apartment, gathering up toothpaste and brushes and T-shirts and magazines and tossing them in the garbage bags Alfie always kept. He threw away clothes and shoes. They didn't have much; when they worked on a job, they packed a suitcase. Still, even the suitcase would be too much to carry.

He leaned over to twist the last bag shut. One of Alfie's shoes was at the top, and for a moment March couldn't see straight. The shoe was just as much his father as a face or a smile, and closing up the bag was like shutting a coffin.

He stuffed it down out of sight.

He walked quietly out of the flat and three blocks down and five blocks over to a construction site. Alfie always picked an apartment that was near major construction, just in case they needed to throw evidence away. He tossed the garbage bag in the Dumpster.

Back at the apartment, he went to the closet and took out Alfie's jacket. Navy flannel, custom tailored, purchased in London on Jermyn Street. March was tall for an almost thirteen-year-old, but the sleeves were too long and he rolled them up. He stuck his hand in a pocket and just came up with a piece of licorice.

He felt along the side of the lining. There was a snap there that concealed a hidden pocket. He put the moonstone inside.

Then he reached for the getaway packs.

Every thief keeps a getaway pack. It's a simple duffel or backpack with enough to get out of town. Just one bag with the right items, in case the police are knocking at the front door and you have to leave by the window.

Alfie had a small nylon duffel, and March had a backpack. He knew what was in his — a change of clothes, a fake passport, about two hundred euros, a disposable cell phone. A toothbrush.

March dumped out the contents of Alfie's duffel on the bed. Fake passport, prepaid cell phone. He grabbed the kit containing toothpaste and soap. He unzipped the top, searched behind the lining, and slid out some bills. American dollars and euros. Total: five thousand dollars.

That couldn't buy him a new life, but it could take him pretty far. *Thanks, Pop.*

There were also items he hadn't expected. A paperback book? Alfie wasn't much of a reader. A pack of playing cards. A key attached to a touristy New York City key chain. Maybe Alfie had a lease on their next apartment somewhere. New York City? Maybe, or maybe he just had a stray key chain. He never told March where they were going until they were in the train station or at the airport.

March used to think that was fun.

Alfie never planned too far ahead. Maybe if he'd been more of a planner, he would have left his son with more than a getaway pack to start over. But Alfie never thought he'd get caught. He'd had a backup plan for every job. Just not the job of father.

March picked up the paperback: *The Moonstone* by

Wilkie Collins, some guy who had been dead for over a hundred years. That was weird. Alfie read newspapers for news, and magazines and websites for tips on what jewels celebrities owned. It was amazing, the information his dad could glean from those fancy home-design magazines, the ones that showed rooms full of furniture but also windows, doors, and room layouts of the rich and famous.

March riffled through the book and a sheet of paper fell out. It was a list in Alfie's handwriting.

1. PARTICLE ZOO
2. ROOM SERVICE
3. VACUUM PACKED
4–5. SURFING MURPH
6. WET PAINT
7. PLASTIC REPLICA

Imaginary band names? March took out his mystified anger on the paper, folding it in quarters and creasing it sharply with a fingernail. He tucked it into the pocket of his jeans. He tossed the book back on the bed. A bookmark fell out. It was a business card. Printed on the front was

THE STICK AND RAG PLAYERS
GUERILLA SPECTACULAR
COMING TO AN ABANDONED SPACE NEAR YOU

Stick, rag, Alfie'd said.

That was what he meant?

Seemed funny that his father would tell him about some group of oddball performers with his last breath.

Talk to me, Pop. What is all this crazy stuff? Getaway packs are supposed to have just enough to get out. Are you trying to tell me something?

No answer, just the faint sounds of a sleeping city coming to life outside his window.

Scrawled on the back of the business card was a street address in Amsterdam, a date, and a time: 10:00 p.m. The date was tomorrow.

March looked out the window at the pink blush on the gray clouds. No. Today.

He glanced at the getaway packs tossed on the bed. He knew that this random stuff had to mean something. It wasn't like Alfie to overpack. He hadn't left these things as a guide for his son. But somehow they would have to be.

He could walk out the door right now. Amsterdam Centraal Station was only blocks away. He could pick a destination, hop on a train. Figure out his next step as the miles took him far away.

Or he could find out what Alfie had been up to.

7

CLOUD SWING

At 9:30 p.m. in the late spring, it was still twilight in Amsterdam.

As March got closer to the address, more people began to fill the streets. Young people streamed from tram stops, scooted around corners, walked in large groups, laughing. He joined the stream heading to the very end of the block, where a small crowd was gathered.

He'd spent the day moving like a ghost. Gliding down backstreets, crossing a street if he felt a glance on his profile, turning a shoulder, hugging a shadow. To be in a crowd unnerved him. He couldn't be sure that there wasn't a figure in a raincoat and black gloves, threading through the people, keeping him in sight.

This couldn't be the address. The warehouse was abandoned, covered in graffiti. There were chains and a padlock on the doors. An old banner, tearing at the edges, was taped across the double doors. It read COMMAND-X.

The sun slanted through the industrial buildings, flashing the bricks with copper. A pale moon hung in the darkening blue sky. He felt as though he were balanced on a hinge between day and night, the knife's edge between one life and another.

The crowd surged and receded. Young people dressed alike in a hodgepodge of circus and punk and old Hollywood glamour. Top hats with fluttering ribbons, fishnet stockings on arms and legs, ripped T-shirts. Girls in tutus over shredded tights, their shoulders and backs inked with dragons and stars and blue moons. Guys in tuxedos with colorful, striped vests. Hair the color of sunsets and Day-Glo posters.

March heard someone speaking English and drifted closer to a trio in their twenties, a girl with electric cobalt-blue hair and two tall boys, one in a neon green cap that read NO LOGO.

"I saw them in Berlin last fall," the girl said.

"Are you sure this is the place? It's so . . . sketchy."

"This is the way it always is," the girl said confidently.

The window flashed red, and for a second, March thought the building was on fire. He took a step back, but the crowd pushed him forward.

The doors burst open, the padlock falling to the ground with a crash.

"It's starting!" the cobalt-haired girl said.

March was a part of the crowd now, helpless in the tide as everyone flowed through the open doors. He was pushed into a vast space. A platform had been set up toward the rear. Two huge blank video screens flanked it. Strings of white and blue lights were woven around metal scaffolding that reached up in the air.

Two men were quickly climbing the metal towers, one on either side of the platform, up to the beam above. The crowd seemed to know what to expect, and it faced the front.

Absolute silence fell as a woman entered from behind a linen curtain, carrying a ukulele. Then the room exploded into applause and cheers, reverberating against the metal and brick. She stood, her chin lifted, giving no sign that she heard.

She was dressed all in midnight blue, in tights and a corset and an artfully frayed velvet frock coat. She wore a top hat that trailed long, tattered pieces of blue silk and net fabric that glittered with crystals.

"It's Blue!" the cobalt-haired girl cried. Her voice cracked with a sob of excitement.

Blue's skin was pale, with a painted blue word running down her cheek. Glancing at the close-up on the screen, March could make it out.

T

E

A

R

Her eyebrows were drawn on her face in high, feathered arches. They gave her an eerily alert expression. Her lipstick was dark and her mouth was wide. Even from here March could see that her wide-set eyes were crystal blue. They glittered.

She held up one hand and the crowd quieted immediately. "Command, control, option, shift," she said. March was surprised to hear her American accent. "We are made of bits and bytes. On our ether pathways, do we grasp the cosmos?" She lifted her hand, and they followed the gesture. Directly above her head, framed in the skylight, was the moon. Just as though she'd summoned it.

She began to strum the ukulele.

"Find the thing you thought you lost
In the place you never look,
While letting go of what it cost,
Holding tight to what you took.
It leaves too fast, it comes too slow,
The space between us is what I know."

Blue dropped the ukulele and lifted her hand. A spotlight appeared and hit a young girl high above them, sitting in a sling made of some kind of fabric. Music blasted through the speakers as the girl leaned forward and the sling began to swing. The girl rocked, back and forth, gaining momentum with each sway. She wrapped her legs around the silk and let go of her hands, and everyone gasped. She spun crazily by her ankles while the audience cheered.

March felt dizzy. The lights, the music, the glittery-eyed woman in the top hat, the girl spinning, his own lack of sleep . . . it all felt like a dream. Pinpoints of white and blue lights began to twirl around them.

Blue climbed the scaffolding and hoisted herself up on the beam. The audience gasped as she threw herself into the air. She had wrapped the fabric around her ankles and she twirled upside down above the ground. The girl tilted backward off the swing and reached out her hands to Blue. Blue pulled herself up until she was level with the young girl again.

The two moved with the rhythm of the tune, entwining themselves again and again in the slender ropes of fabric as they swung upside down and then right side up and back again.

"It's like every dream I ever had," the cobalt-haired girl breathed.

"Or nightmare," her friend said.

That was when they heard the sirens.

8

HERE IS THE BOY

The audience stirred, and March caught Blue's reaction as she just missed grabbing the girl's hand. Keeping to the rhythm of the music, she pulled herself up, somersaulted through the air, and landed on the ground. She stood, hands on her hips, and waited.

The spotlight shut off, and the police came in with whistles and authority. The audience began to boo and call out in different languages.

"Please to file out," an officer called in English. "No permit, no show."

The grumbling increased, but no one wanted to be arrested, and there was a general but slow move toward the exits. Blue went over to the police and began to argue. March tried to lose himself in the crowd, but he felt himself being pushed toward the stage. Somehow he wound up standing with the crew and the performers. The young girl idly swung over their heads, occasionally twining her feet into the sling and flipping lazily upside down.

"Get down off that swing!" the policeman yelled at her in Dutch, then German, then English, as though if he hit the right language, she would obey.

She swung back and forth, just looking at him. Then in a terrific display of strength and agility, she pulled herself up, swung over his head, then flipped over, hung by her heels, grabbed on to a trapeze bar March hadn't noticed, and swung herself to land exactly three inches in front of him. The policeman stumbled backward. The girl grinned.

"English," Blue said to the policeman. "Speak English. Yes, I know, but you wouldn't *give* me a permit, and the show must go on. Do you know that expression?"

March was so intent on watching Blue — actually it was hard to take your eyes off her — that he hadn't noticed an officer standing off to the side, who was staring at him. March recognized his mustache with a sinking feeling. He had been there last night.

Every muscle tensed, but he told himself to keep himself loose. He pretended to search the crowd, balancing on his toes, and then moved forward as if he'd spotted someone.

Too late. The policeman blocked him.

He spoke to him in a pleasant tone. "What is your name, please?"

"Matt Henneberry."

If you're on the spot, and there's a chance to get away, give a last name that sounds nonthreatening but doesn't sound made-up. And add a friendly first name.

"You were there last night," the cop said.

"Where?" March asked.

The policeman didn't answer. "You are here alone?"

"I'm here with my mom. She's a big fan. I lost her in the crowd." March pretended to crane his neck. "But I see her! So —"

"You are staying in Amsterdam? What hotel?"

Always give them an American hotel. And smile. Americans in Europe always smile at cops.

"The Hilton."

Now make them an offer. You don't have to follow through.

"My mom's probably looking for me outside." He held up his cell phone. "I can text her; she can come back and meet you." March started to back away, hiding his desperation behind a grin and a waving cell phone. "I'll be right back —"

The policeman's eyes were gray steel and looked older than his face. "Let's have her find you, shall we?"

No matter how good you are, kid, remember this: Sometimes you get caught.

9

LONG LOST

Munching on a bag of chips, March watched people walk by, attached to huge suitcases they would shortly try to stuff into overhead compartments. People would argue and then finally settle into their seats and wait for free snacks.

All airports were alike. Everybody was in a big hurry and a bad mood. Hurry to get away and leave their problems, hurry to get home and face them again.

The destination sign read NEW YORK. The American official sat next to him, his thick, sweaty arm parked on March's armrest.

Child Protective Services in the U.S. had been called, and he was being sent to what was called a group home in upstate New York. March didn't know what the "group" was, and he figured that "home" was aspirational.

The official had told March his name when they'd met this morning, but March kept forgetting it. What he did remember was that, within five minutes, the guy had told him he'd break his fingers one by one if March tried to run away.

March knew he was a peach of a guy within fifteen minutes, when the official had confiscated his cell phone and found his stash of cash behind the lining of his toiletry kit. Then he pocketed it.

"I'll have to confiscate this," he said.

"Where's my receipt?" March asked.

"Smart guy," he responded.

March knew he'd never see the money again.

Maybe "protective" was aspirational, too.

The official pored over a car magazine, his mouth moving with the crazy rhythm of Juicy Fruit. What was his name? Creydon or Crayfrun or Reydun or Raygun, or should March just call him Mr. Soda? He had a little cooler at his feet, and kept taking out cans. He'd already had three Diet Pepsis and it was barely 10:00 a.m. His conversation was sprinkled with a series of belches and hiccups.

One of the airline guys made the announcement that they'd board in five. It was March's last chance to run.

Important to know when you're beaten. Just hang, and wait for your next chance. At least he'd get a free ticket to the States. It would be easier to get lost there.

He'd had a week before they figured out the paperwork and made the phone calls and decided where he was going. A week to think about why Alfie had sent him to the Stick and Rag. Was there someone he was supposed to meet there? Someone holding jewels for Alfie? If that was true, he'd blown it.

Mr. Soda looked at his watch and snapped his magazine. "Where are they? We're going to board soon." *Burp.* "I want to get the overhead compartment."

"Who's 'they'?" he asked, but the guy didn't answer. "Gosh, I love these meaningful talks of ours," March added. The official continued to ignore him.

March glanced out the window at the tarmac. It was raining lightly, the soft silver rain he'd come to know in his three weeks in Holland. Somewhere in the cold belly of the plane was a small box. In that box was what remained of Alfie McQuin.

The official had called the box the cremains. March detested the word. It made it sound like they'd turned his pop into a zombie. Or a breakfast cereal.

March stared out at the rain. An airport was the loneliest place in the world if you didn't have a home.

Mr. Soda stood up. "I'm not waiting any longer. Let's board."

Just then another official hurried toward them, a woman busting out of her blue shirt and blazer. At her side was a slender, tall girl March's age, dressed in black jeans and a hoodie. Another orphan, or a runaway, he guessed. She had that desperate vibe. Just like him, he supposed. Now he was a member of that invisible crowd: the kids nobody wanted.

The girl had black hair cut very short and wary gray eyes that shifted from Mr. Soda to March. She looked familiar, and it was with a sense of dumbfounded shock that March realized that she was the girl who'd performed on the swing a week before.

"Time you two met, I guess," Mr. Soda said. "Julia, meet March. Your long-lost" — *burp* — "brother."

March and the girl didn't look at each other. They looked at the official, uncertain whether he was joking.

"Oh gosh, look at that," the woman said. "You can see they're related, cantcha? You both have the same expression. Didn't they tell you about each other?"

Sister?

10

BLUE TEARS

March felt like a needle spinning on a compass in a world suddenly without true north.

The girl eyed him warily. She looked just as rocked as he did.

She — Julia — narrowed her eyes at him, and suddenly he saw Alfie in her face. Something in the way her mouth turned down as she concentrated.

His sister.

"You're twins," the woman official said. "The kind who don't look alike. Is that fraternal or . . . what's the other word?"

"Doomed?" Julia asked.

He saw anger flicker in her eyes. But was it for him or the officials? Or Alfie?

Alfie, who had told him everything? Except this *most important thing*?

Twins. They had the same coloring. Black hair, gray eyes that sometimes looked blue.

Every birthday he had, every year with every present, every special dinner, there was a daughter Alfie had been thinking of, too.

March was desperate to run. Fast as he could, weaving through the suitcases and the tote bags and the newspapers and the cups of coffee and all these faces, all these people, so he could get to a place that was quiet and still. So he could think.

"Time to board," Mr. Soda said. "Those two have plenty of time to get acquainted."

How do you get acquainted with a twin you never even knew existed? Where do you start? *Who was your favorite, Bert or Ernie? Trucks or dolls? Peanut butter or jam?*

Alfie had plenty to answer for.

The thought had rushed in so quickly, and now again the hole opened up, the place where he knew Alfie wasn't here anymore to get mad at.

They heard the sound of a sudden commotion behind them.

Someone shouted, "Wait!"

Blue rushed through the crowd. She was dressed half in her performance attire, the velvet frock coat over jeans. Her eyes were rimmed in makeup that had smeared, and a real tear rolled down the blue-lettered *tear*.

"Jewels!"

Julia turned.

Blue stopped. "Jules," she said. The word was a sigh.

Not *jewels*. *Jules*. A nickname for Julia.

Find jewels.

No. Find *Jules*.

The knowledge ripped through March. Alfie wasn't tipping him off to a fortune, but a *person*. *That's* why he'd sent him to the Stick and Rag.

He *wanted* him to find her.

Blue walked forward and put her hands on Jules's cheeks. "I was arrested. I just got out. They wouldn't let me say good-bye to you. How could they stop me from saying good-bye?"

"Ma'am . . ." the official said. "We really have to go."

Blue ignored him. "They said I'm not a fit parent. I'm your *aunt*."

If Jules was his sister, that meant that Blue was his aunt, too. Was she Alfie's sister? Or his mother's? It was like hearing a pink flamingo was related to him. This exotic creature, this person in a velvet coat with fishnet stockings on her arms and tattoos, was his *aunt*?

"I raised you!" Blue shot a dark and terrible glance at the officials. "Now suddenly I don't know what I'm doing?"

"Ms. Barnes, we've got nothing to do with this. Just following orders. And we've got to go," the official said, taking Jules by the arm.

March expected Jules to shake the man off and turn to Blue, but she didn't. She seemed frozen.

Barnes. His mother's last name. This was his mother's sister. And he never knew. Alfie told him the family was dead, or scattered.

Texas or Canada, Alfie?

Why did you keep this secret from me?

Blue grabbed Jules tighter. "No! You can't take her!"

The airline employee spoke into a phone. Security was on the way.

Blue grabbed at Jules's backpack. "Jules!" she cried, pulling at it, as though she could yank Jules backward into the life they'd had. "Run!"

Jules still didn't move. She sucked in her lower lip and bit it hard.

Two muscled security officers grabbed Blue by her arms. They force-marched her away.

Jules rubbed her fist against her cheek like a little girl might do. She hunched her shoulders, pulled up her hood, and turned her face toward the plane.

11

JOKERS WILD

Somewhere in the middle of the Atlantic Ocean, the two officials fell asleep while watching a movie and drinking scotch.

"Why not?" Mr. Soda said, pouring the liquid from the miniature bottle into his can. "We have a" — *burp* — "per diem!"

March would have liked to sleep, too. It was just that lately he'd had this recurring nightmare about falling. He was climbing a cliff high above a body of water. Sometimes he was trying desperately to snatch at a hand. He could feel the grit of the rock against his palms and scraping against his cheek. He always woke up before hitting the black water.

He didn't think death by falling was a great dream to have on a plane.

He took out *The Moonstone* and the pack of playing cards, and placed them on his tray table. Jules had her earbuds in and was flipping through a magazine. He saw her watching him out of the corner of her eye.

"Per diem?" March asked her.

She removed one earbud, and March repeated the question.

"An amount they can spend every day for food and stuff. We're their meal ticket, basically."

"Well, the big one stole my wad of cash," March said. "Five grand I'm not getting back. I should have hit him with a can of soda."

She took out the other earbud. Things were improving. "Yeah, that would have solved everything."

"It would have given me satisfaction."

"Piece of advice for you — never start a fight you can't win."

March shook his head. "You sound like Alfie."

"I doubt it," Jules said. Her lips pressed together. "I didn't know he was my father until a couple of months ago."

"How often did you see him?" he asked. How much of a secret life did Alfie have?

"Only once in a while. He'd show up occasionally at whatever pitch we'd managed to scrounge up."

"Pitch?"

"The place street performers stake out," she explained. "We started out in public squares, but then when Blue got the idea of the cloud swing, we moved into abandoned places where we could set up the rigging. We sometimes try to get a permit, but usually it's easier not to. Plus the audience likes it better if they think they're doing something illegal. Blue calls it guerilla spectacle."

"So Alfie would just turn up sometimes?"

"Blue said he was a friend. I didn't ask questions." She rubbed her knuckle along her lower lip. "When you live like I did, it's better not to know things."

He knew what Jules meant. He'd lived with a thief. Alfie would leave him alone for stretches of time, leave him with instructions and cash and a smile, and then show up again one day, sometimes tossing the cash on the bed and saying, *Easy street, kid!*

But Alfie had never asked and March had never volunteered how scary that time alone had been.

Berlin last fall, the girl with the cobalt hair had said. Alfie had traveled there for a few days, casing a job he was thinking about. He said. Had he been there for the Stick and Rag? How many of those times that he'd left March in an apartment for days at a stretch — how often was he really seeing Jules?

How many lies?

You've never let me down, March.

He saw his father sitting in a pool of light in an armchair by March's bed.

I wish I could say the same about myself. There's things I haven't told you.

What had March said? They'd been talking because he'd been afraid to go back to sleep. He'd had the nightmare. This time he'd told Alfie about it. He'd liked how his pop had taken the dream seriously, asked him questions about it, even looked as shaken as March felt.

Then he'd dragged over an armchair, close to the bed, saying he'd stay up until March fell asleep again. And even though March was way too old for this, he hadn't said no.

After this job, we'll blow town, head for the States. I've got things to tell you. Show you. It's time.

Was Alfie getting ready to tell him about Jules? Was he going to clear up all the lies?

Or just tell another?

March tapped the deck and it fell out of its package into his hand. He fished out the jokers. One was ripped in half and he tossed it on his tray table. He held up the deck. "Poker?"

"Sure . . ." Jules's voice trailed off as she stared at the joker.

"What's the matter?"

"That card." She leaned over to fish inside her backpack. She brought out a playing card, ripped in half. A joker.

March picked up his half. Holding his breath, he held it out. Jules's half met his. They matched perfectly.

12

PLAYING FOR PRETZELS

"I got it from Alfie," Jules said. "The last time I saw him. He said he had something special for me."

"Special?"

"I said, 'It's just a torn-up card.' He said I had to learn how to appreciate a lucky piece. He said, 'Keep it in your pocket. Never let it go.' Figure I needed luck, so . . ."

They stared at the joker, both halves joined.

"Some joke," she said.

"It's so we could recognize each other, right? Like something out of a fairy tale."

Jules snorted. "So this is happily ever after?"

March shuffled the cards. He pushed them toward her to cut the deck. "He told you he was your father?" he asked.

"More like I guessed. He'd always bring me presents — little things. He got me these puppets from Germany once. Chocolates. A bunch of silk violets. Just a month ago he bought me a sewing machine — I do all the costumes for the troupe."

March shook out his bag of pretzels. He divided them up. "Chips. Ante up."

She pushed a pretzel forward, he matched it, and then dealt five cards down. Alfie had taught him poker, and March had never been able to beat him. Alfie had shown him the most important things, like how to spot a tell — an indication of how a player might bid — and how to look for crooks. *Never cheat, but be able to spot a cheater.*

Jules frowned at her cards. "Anyway, the last time I saw him was last week, the day we got to Amsterdam. Blue had a bunch of sites to check out for the pitch. They had this long argument — I don't know what about. I could only see their faces — I was in the caravan. Alfie left, and I ran after him. I just knew suddenly. Why did he keep coming around? I knew it wasn't for Blue. So I just said it to him, 'Hey, are you my dad?' He started to bawl and said yes, that he'd explain everything, but I said I didn't need any explanations. He asked me what I wanted for my thirteenth birthday. I said a turntable and some vinyl. He said he'd give me something better. A home." Jules grimaced. "Well, he was right about that, wasn't he? A group home with a bunch of juvenile delinquents." She pushed two pretzels into the pot.

"Wonder why he kept us apart," March said.

"Probably because two kids slow down a crook."

March glanced at her sharply, but she stared at her cards. He had a lousy hand, but he had a two and a four of diamonds. The chances of a straight weren't great, but he might as well go for broke. All he had to lose was a snack. "See your two pretzels and raise you two."

She threw two cards down. "Do you think we'll have to go to school?"

He dealt her two more. "I'd say that's a given."

"Stinks. I wonder if we'll have to take tests. What are you supposed to know at twelve? Geometry?" She rubbed her knuckle against her lip. It was a tell, he decided. She did it when she was nervous.

"I know how to pick locks, but I don't think that's a subject. Dealer takes three." March held the cards without looking at them. "He told me that, for my birthday, we were going to stay put for a long while. He must have been planning something."

Right before the job, Alfie had seemed nervous. He'd smiled and said, *Some jobs have higher stakes, buddy. This is one.*

Jules gave a dismissive shrug. "Guys like him are always full of plans. And the plans usually revolve around them." She looked at him, her gray eyes glinting like silver. "Our dad was a liar and a thief. Face it. He handed me off to Blue when I was two, like I was a package he was sick of carrying." She fanned out her cards. "Four of a kind!"

His eyes burning, March stared at his cards. It took a minute for the numbers and shapes to make sense. He felt a surge of triumph as he threw down his cards.

"He wasn't a liar. Straight flush!" He scooped up the handful of pretzels and crunched down on one. "And maybe he had a reason!"

Her cheeks were red. "What kind of reason do you need to have to give away your own kid? I notice he kept *you*."

"He said he went crazy after our mother died —"

"What are you, the excuser in chief?"

"He's just not as bad as you think!"

"And maybe he's not as good as you say!"

Angrily, March gathered the cards from the tray table. Jules clamped her hand on his wrist.

"Wait a second."

She picked up the top card from March's pile. She peered at it. When she looked at him, her gaze was pure fury. "These cards are marked! You cheated!"

13

GROWN-UPS LIE

March looked down at the card. The design on the back was of a city skyline: black-and-white buildings with little white boxes for windows. On two of his cards, numbers were written in the boxes in a kind of pattern, penciled in lightly.

"I didn't know," March said. He flipped over the card. The five of diamonds.

"Sure. Son of a thief didn't know the cards were marked. Tell me another one." Jules rolled her eyes at him.

March felt heat rise in his cheeks. "I never looked at these cards! Alfie left them behind."

"Then he was a thief and a liar *and* a cheater!"

"Say what you want," he said, furious. "I don't care. I don't even *know* you. But think about this. He said he'd give you a home. He said the same thing to me. He must have been planning something. Some big score. He must have wanted us all to be together."

"You're delusional." Jerkily, she grabbed her earbuds. "Let me give you a tip — grown-ups lie."

She put her earbuds back in, cranked up her volume, and closed her eyes.

March regarded her through a red mist of fury. He couldn't put the word *sister* next to this girl who just happened to have the same parents as his. She had three earrings in one ear and wore a ring on her thumb. Her hands looked rough and calloused. She could twist her body into shapes and swing fifty feet in the air. She'd had a whole life he couldn't imagine. Her irritability level was off the charts.

And she hated their dad.

Hated March now, too, apparently.

What did he expect, instant family?

March turned away. He flipped through the deck. Six cards had notations on the backs, from the two of diamonds on up. Random numbers that made no sense. Just like the random phrases on Alfie's list.

Alfie wasn't a cheater. He knew that. So what did the numbers mean?

Exhaustion crashed down on him. He put the flimsy pillow against his cheek and leaned back. The cards blurred on the tray table as his eyes closed. He remembered Alfie's face when he said, *I've got things to tell you.* He wished he'd been more awake. He wished he'd said, *Tell me now.*

What were you planning, Pop?

14

SO LONG, ALFIE

In lots of ways that people usually counted, March had probably had a lousy life. No roots laid down, no best friend, no school prizes, no Saturday soccer games where he'd kicked the winning goal. Weird to have your dad be your best friend. And *Alfie's* friends — well, they weren't exactly role models. His babysitter Penelope was a grifter. His "uncle" Ham taught him math at the racetrack.

But still, Alfie tried to make it fun when he could. After a big job, they'd check into a good hotel and have a spree. The holiday in Turkey or Hong Kong or that time they stayed in the Maldive Islands in the Indian Ocean for three weeks — *They're sinking, I hear, so we'd better go now, kid! I don't want there to be one place in the world you can't go.*

Don't call me kid, Pop.

Okay, kid.

But it was his life, and he didn't want to be here, standing in a cemetery over an open grave. He missed his father so much that he couldn't breathe.

The two social workers who had picked them up at the airport stood by, reluctant mourners who kept checking their watches. They were the administrators of the group home they were heading to, called Polestar House. Mandy Sue Miller was short and peppy, with a steady hum of irritability ("Gosh, you took so long at customs — are you smugglers, ha-ha?") underneath a wide smile and cheeks so round, March was positive she was storing nuts inside them. Pete Campos was tall and restless.

He was thin, she was plump; she was chatty, he was silent; and no doubt, between them, they licked the platter clean.

Jules just looked as though she wanted to be anywhere but here.

"Thruway traffic and whatnot," Pete whispered to Mandy Sue. He jiggled the car keys in his pocket. "Let's get this show on the road."

The cemetery guy coughed. "Do you have anything to say?" he asked.

"I hardly knew him," Jules said. "Thanks for nothing, Dad."

March curled his hands into fists. All he could see was the box, the hole, the plain marker. Birth, death, and nothing in between to show his dad had a life.

Alfie never looked back. *Humans aren't meant to look back. Or else we'd be able to turn our heads in a 180, just like an owl.* He was always looking ahead to the next city, the next adventure. Maybe even now he was shooting forward somewhere in that other dimension, eyes wide open and looking for his chance. No 180s for Alfie, not even now.

"Don't look back," March blurted.

Mandy Sue gave him a shocked look. "Godresthissoul, oh Lord," she said in a tone that indicated that March was a heathen.

"Amen," Pete said, and glanced at his watch again.

March kept his gaze well away from the dirt that was now being shoveled over his father and saw a man leaning against a tree, not looking at them. He was wearing a fedora pulled low over his forehead.

Alfie had taught him that there were people who didn't look at you and then there were people who *deliberately* didn't look at you, and it was crucial to know the difference.

The guy was there for him.

15

PARTY CRASHERS

The man must have noticed that March was now deliberately not looking at *him*, and so he walked down the cemetery road as if he had a pressing engagement with a dead person.

March remembered the person in the raincoat, standing on that corner in Amsterdam, whistling. Same guy? That would just be too creepy. But . . .

A minute later a green Audi barreled down the road.

Mandy Sue and Pete huddled with the cemetery manager. Mandy Sue tapped on her clipboard with a pointed pink fingernail. "Well, I need the paperwork *today*. You don't know what it's like, dealing with state government! If I don't have it, I'm up poo creek without a paddle, ha-ha! No joke!"

She turned to March and Jules and said with bright ferocity, "Do *not* go anywhere! I can see you from that window!"

The three of them stumped off toward the office. March looked across the grave markers at Jules, who was now sitting on the grass, staring down at her shoes.

"Great eulogy," he said. "Thanks."

She looked up, startled at the anger in his voice. "What was I supposed to say?"

"How about, *I'm sorry*," March shot back. His voice was suddenly choked, and he could feel his face growing hot. "I just buried my *father*, okay? You didn't love him, I *get* that. But I . . ."

The words left him with the breath that wouldn't come. The words *I did.* They were in the air between them. His *love* was between them. Exposed. That love was his, not hers. It was his to hold, his to hide. From now on. For the rest of his life. There would be no one who would know it. No one he would tell. Only Alfie had heard it, had held it, and he was gone. To his horror, March felt tears in his throat. He wanted to punch a tree.

"Ever since this happened," he said, his voice shaking, "I want someone to say, 'I'm sorry.' And mean it."

Jules stood unsteadily, her hands jammed in her pockets. "Okay," she said. "Okay. I get it. I'm sorry. I really am," she added. "I know I've been lousy. You just can't help hating someone who never wanted you."

"He gave you up," March said. "But that doesn't mean he didn't want you."

She scowled and kicked a stone. "What's the difference?"

A large black Hummer with tinted windows crested the hill. It drove off the road and over the gravestones that laid flat in the earth. It rolled to a stop only a few feet from them.

The tinted window slid down. An older woman with black hair and wraparound sunglasses stuck her head out. March turned away, hiding his wet eyes.

"Did I miss it?" she asked.

"I think you've got the wrong funeral, lady," Jules said.

She took off her sunglasses and leaned out the window. "You have your father's eyes," she said to Jules.

March turned. The woman was staring at both of them. Powder settled into the wrinkles around her eyes and mouth. Her lipstick was orange and slick.

"Said he was an insurance salesman. Broke into my house just to show me he could, so he could sell me a policy.

I showed him everything — the jewels, the security . . . what a fool I was. Charming man, your father."

"I didn't know him that well," Jules said. "Thanks for coming."

"He stole more than riches," the woman said. Her hands clutched the wheel. Her fingers were long, with knobby knuckles and blue veins. "He stole my *future*."

"Right," Jules said. "But he's dead now, so —"

She stuck out a bony finger and pointed to Alfie's grave. "He's where he belongs!"

Before March could react, Jules jackknifed to her feet. In one leap she was up against the car door. "You want to try that one again, crazy lady? Show some respect."

Now she was defending Alfie? March looked on, startled at Jules's sudden fierceness.

Rattled, the woman put her sunglasses back on. "If I were you, I'd show some respect. I'm here to offer you a deal."

"What kind of deal?" March asked.

"What did he leave you?"

"What business is it of yours?"

She fixed her watery blue eyes on March. "Because I want them back. The moonstones. They are rough magic. Cruel. But real." She extended a clawlike hand. "Beware of them!"

A voice came yodeling out across the distance. "Maaarrch! Juliiiiaa! Get in the carrrrr!" It was Mandy Sue.

"I'll find you again," she hissed. Jules had to leap back as the big car jerked forward, bumping over the gravestones and taking off down Cemetery Road.

"Crazy old bat," Jules said.

"Yeah," March said. His hand found the secret pocket and closed around the moonstone.

16

HOME SWEET DUMP

Crazy old ladies and magic moonstones flew right out of March's head as Pete pulled up a pockmarked driveway to their new home.

Two houses crouched on a plot of chartreuse lawn. One was a noxious shade of antacid pink and the other was the color of a bruise. A sad little swing hung from the branch of a monster oak. The garage looked like it would collapse if a hummingbird landed on it. There was a surprisingly healthy vegetable garden in the back.

"Welcome to Polestar House! Pink for girls, blue for boys," Mandy Sue said. "Get it? I picked the colors myself. Bubble gum and blueberry, ha-ha."

"Classic," Jules said. "Ha-ha."

Mandy Sue twisted in the front seat to look at Jules. Her smile was brightly false. "Okay, throw your packs and duffels down on the ground!" she trilled.

"Is there a bellhop?" March asked.

"Bedbugs," Mandy Sue said. "Nobody gets in my house with their suitcases until I make sure you're not carrying any little hitchhikers with ya! I seal up the luggage in plastic bags and then stick 'em in the deep freeze for two days."

"I don't . . . have . . . bedbugs," Jules said.

"But you lived on the street, riiigggght?"

"No, I lived in a caravan." Jules's voice was made of ice. "We were a traveling troupe. In the off-season I lived in a house. Just like you."

"And I lived in an apartment," March said. "The landlady cleaned every day."

"There are clean clothes and a changing area in the garage. I'll put your stuff in sealable bags. Rules! Pete, your turn." Mandy Sue headed off to the pink house.

"Rules," Pete said. "Better get used to following them. It will make things so much easier."

"For you?" Jules asked.

"For you," Pete said. "I promise you that."

March changed into bright-green sweatpants that were too short and a T-shirt that advertised Mountain Dew. He looked like an overgrown leprechaun.

He stood by a splintery picnic table and looked at the back of the house. How was it possible that he'd traveled halfway around the world and ended up here in Dumpsville?

A window rattled open on the second floor, and a boy stuck his head out. He held his dreadlocks back with one hand as he let out a long gob of spit. March watched as it hit the walk just inches from his sneakers.

"Cuke Boy!" the boy yelled, and slammed the window down.

Rats would check out of this dump.

I know, Pop.

If there's no way out, find a way.

I know.

17

UP POO CREEK

And now for the grand tour. He joined Jules, who was standing with Pete. She was dressed in a T-shirt with a lollipop on the front and pink sweats.

"Don't say a word," she warned him.

Every piece of furniture was dinged, scuffed, or torn. There were locks on the closets and locks on the fridge. Peppy posters lined the halls, which said BE YOURSELF, NO ONE ELSE CAN and TRY TRY TRY UNTIL YOU DO DO DO.

"Mandy makes up the sayings and prints them on the computer," Pete said. "She's got a real talent."

"Clearly," Jules said.

March smelled antiseptic and something underneath that. Onions? Pine? Cherry mouthwash? "What is that smell?" he whispered to Jules.

"It's the scent of 'nobody cares,' " she answered.

Pete was especially proud of the "hangout room," a paneled and ultrasueded den that smelled like mildew and popcorn, with a stained green carpet and two couches wrapped in plastic. "Mandy Sue has got a thing about bugs," he said. He pointed to the new acquisition, a flat-screen TV.

"We have television nights on Saturdays and occasional important sports events," Pete said. "Super Bowl and whatnot. Counselors have to approve the choice of program, and there's a discussion of what program to watch. Majority rules."

March noted a round hole in the drywall, about the size of a fist.

"Sometimes the discussion can get heated," Pete said.

"Can't wait," March said.

"'Kay. Rules. Four p.m. to six p.m., that's quiet time — for homework and whatnot. Lights-out nine thirty p.m. Doors are locked after ten p.m. No entering the pink house next door, ever, without permission. Mandy Sue and I will work out a schedule so you two can see each other."

Jules shifted. March looked at the hole in the wall. Did they *want* to see each other? Could he escape this place without her? Leave her behind?

He thought of Alfie's fluttering hand. *Find Jules. . . .*

"'Kay. Julia, Mandy Sue is waiting for you in the pink house. March, come with me."

March followed behind Pete. He led him to a whiteboard at the back door, a chart with all the boys' names written down and a series of boxes next to them labeled GOALS. Under that category were listed things like CHORES, HOMEWORK COMPLETED, POSITIVE ATTITUDE! and GARDEN.

"Everybody's got to work in the garden," Pete said. "It's Mandy Sue's thing."

March quickly scanned the whiteboard. Most of the kids had a bunch of green and yellow checks, with a few reds sprinkled in. All except for a kid named Darius Fray. Who had a line of red checks next to his name.

"Green means you're toeing the line," Pete said.

March had never met a line he hadn't wanted to cross.

"Yellow means *caution, buddy, you're in my sight line.* Red means you've got one foot into juvie land. A total of twenty checks, you're out — sent back into the system, which I guarantee will not be a picnic."

March counted nineteen checks in Darius's column. Most of them were under POSITIVE ATTITUDE! He saw the phrase AGGRESSIVE BEHAVIOR!!!!!!! He counted the exclamation points. "So who's the psycho?"

"That would be me," a deep voice said.

18

FRANKENBOOT

March turned to find the boy he'd seen spitting out the window earlier.

Darius was a six-foot tower of muscle topped with shoulder-length dreads. He had feet like canoes and hands like Easter hams. One swipe and March would face-plant in New Jersey.

Darius took in March's floppy green sweats and Mountain Dew T-shirt. "So this is Cuke Boy," he said. "Welcome."

The words were perfectly normal. But the gaze said *death.*

"Darius, meet March, your new roommate," Pete said.

He gave him a lazy smile. "Looks like you get the psycho, bro. Boo!"

Pete held up a finger. "That's enough. You've run out of options, big fella. After what happened to the last roommate . . . no funny business!"

"Aw, what's a couple of visits to the ER?" Darius asked. He winked at March. "And this one doesn't look as accident-prone."

March took in a gulp of air. *First sign of a bully, you have to go for it. If you wait, you're dead. You might still be breathing, but it's all over. You're that guy's puppy dog from then on.*

"Aside from that excess saliva problem, I'm sure we'll get along," he said.

Darius tilted his head. He regarded March the way a lion might eye a gazelle, planning the fun of running it down before ripping its throat open.

Outside the kitchen window March noticed a tiny girl with pigtails and an adorable face watching the encounter. When she saw him notice her, she smiled, two deep dimples appearing in her cheeks. Then she leaned closer and pointed at Darius, then March. Still smiling, she mouthed the words as she drew a finger across her throat:

You're dead.

It was like waiting for the other shoe to drop. A Frankenstein boot of doom.

The suspense was killing March. Darius didn't even flick his gaze once at him during dinner. Bedtime rituals began at nine, and lights-out was at nine thirty. March brushed his teeth and flicked out his light at nine fifteen. He heard the lonesome hoot of the commuter train as it approached the station a half mile away. He imagined running for it.

Instead he lay awake and waited to be killed.

At nine thirty Pete yelled, "Lights-out!" and the lights flicked off, one by one. March lay rigid.

The floorboards creaked. An immense shadow expanded to fill the bed.

March climbed out of bed. He was fully dressed.

He held up a hand. "Dude. I realize you're older, taller, and meaner than I am. And you possibly have a chemical imbalance. But let's be clear. I'm not going to be your puppy in this kennel. So. What are we going to do?"

Darius's voice vibrated more with melancholy than menace, as if he were deeply sad at the damage he was about to inflict on March's person. He stared down at him with hooded eyes. "Well, lookit you, Scooby-Doo," he said. "Let's take a walk. You and I are about to have a . . . conversation."

Every nerve was skittering as he followed Darius down the back staircase. Alfie had instructed him to get the first punch in, but March had never punched anybody. Why hadn't Alfie told him where to *aim*?

Pete's office door was closed, but a thin line of yellow light showed at the door frame. They moved silently past it.

Darius stopped at the back door. It was fastened with a padlock.

"Open it."

March wanted to pretend he didn't know how, but he had a feeling that wouldn't fly. He didn't know how Darius knew he was good with locks, but he wasn't about to bluff.

Alfie had taught him how to make a shim with assorted handy things — a soda can, a bobby pin, a paper clip. Next to the whiteboard was a bulletin board. March found the chore schedule, which was paper clipped together. He took the paper clip, straightened it, and wiggled the end into the padlock. He turned it, and when he felt the tumblers move and click into place, he bent the paper clip and used the tension to pull it to the right. The lock sprang open.

It had taken him about five seconds. Darius raised an eyebrow.

How smart was it to pick the lock to your very own doom? No choice. March pushed open the door to Mayhem City.

19

LET'S MAKE A DEAL

His heart now hammering triple time, March followed Darius down the dark lawn, their footsteps whispering in the grass.

Something alerted him, some sense of movement or sound, and March whipped around in time to see a shadow detach from the roof next door. Someone landed on the wide flat branch of the oak and reached out to swing a smaller shadow down.

Jules and the tiny girl who had told him he was going to die.

Jules lowered the other girl to the garage roof. The girl inched along to the edge while Jules kicked out with her feet to send the swing wide. Then she grabbed it, flipped over, swung hard, and, hanging on to the two ropes, did a double somersault to the ground.

"Whoa," Darius said.

She went to the garage roof, climbed up a drainpipe, and waited for the small kid to climb on her back. Then she slid to the ground.

"Hey," she said. She folded her arms, addressing Darius. "How long?"

"About five seconds, including straightening the paper clip," Darius said.

"Toldja," Jules said.

So Jules was the one who told the freak that he could pick locks. Betrayed already. And they'd only just met.

Still, it looked as though she saved him from a Jersey face-plant, so . . .

"Meet Izzy," Darius said, indicating the petite girl. "We've got a deal on the table."

"And that is?" March asked warily.

"You pick locks. That brings up opportunities for advancement."

"What do you have in mind?"

"This is a corrupt system, and I want to maximize my experience," Darius said, tilting back and crossing his arms. "One way or another, I'll be out of here and on the streets, and if I have a stake, I'll be better off."

"What do you mean, a corrupt system?"

"You notice how beat every stick of furniture is? How everybody fights over the food, bad as it is? Mandy Sue and Pete are skimming off the top. Scamming the state. What did we have for dinner tonight?"

"Um, gray meat and canned corn?"

"You see that vegetable garden? Mandy Sue found this organization that gives out grants to people who plant organic gardens for at-risk kids. So we weed it, and she takes pictures of us. Then she sells the produce to the farmers' market and pockets the cash. Corrupt system, bro."

"So what's your idea?"

"Mandy Sue goes across the river to the big-box store and buys everything in bulk," Darius said. "I know a guy who operates out of his trailer. Sells stuff that fell off a truck for cheap."

"Stuff that fell off a truck? You mean it was stolen."

Darius shrugged. "We can get an exchange going."

"Toilet paper and laundry detergent?" March tried to

keep the disdain out of his voice, but, really. He'd gone from assisting a diamond heist to *toilet paper*?

"Don't knock it," Darius said. "It's cash in your pocket. All you have to do is pick a lock."

"Won't she notice stuff is missing?"

Darius pointed with his chin. "Izzy here fixes Pete's computer, runs his programs. She can change the amounts in the inventory. She's got his password."

"How'd you get good at hacking, Izzy?" Jules asked.

Izzy shrugged. Her face seemed to close down.

"Izzy doesn't like to talk unless she has something to say," Darius said. "Things go better for you here if you shut up." He grinned. "Unfortunately I can't seem to stay on that particular path."

Jules eased herself off the picnic table. "I hear you, Darius," she said. "It's a tough break for all of us, landing here. Especially considering Mandy Sue's taste in sweatpants. But the way I look at it, we've got three squares a day and a bed to sleep in. Maybe a foster family down the line. I've spent my whole life moving. I'm ready to stay put."

Darius guffawed. "You're looking at a *foster family* to save you? Talk to Izzy sometime about the swell folks she met up with in the system."

"So you won't help us?" Izzy's voice was small.

"Sorry," Jules said. "I know I used to swing on a trapeze for a living, but I don't steal." She smirked at March. "That's more my brother's line."

20

THEY GOT AWAY WITH IT!

The next night Darius found him trying to read *The Moonstone* in his room.

"TV night, Marcello. Lame, but it cuts the despair."

March followed Darius down the stairs. Kids thundered through the halls, slammed doors, skidded in their socks. In the den, they jostled for the best positions. Jules was already there, sitting on the floor with Izzy. The room was pretty much divided between boys and girls, and it would look weird if he sat next to her. Not that he wanted to. He sat against the wall.

Pete and Mandy Sue had commandeered the armchairs. Mandy Sue was flossing her teeth.

"Just don't look," Darius whispered. "And watch out for flying corn."

Pete stood up, holding the remote. "Anybody doesn't follow the rules, it goes off," he said. He held the remote for a few seconds longer, just to let them know who was boss. Then he turned on the TV.

One by one the words splattered in lurid red type across the screen.

THEY

GOT

AWAY

WITH

IT!

WITH YOUR HOST

DETECTIVE MIKE SHANNON

Mist blanketed an alley. A man strode toward the camera in a belted trench coat and fedora.

"Loser!" someone yelled.

"Detective Stupid!"

"Pipe down!" Mandy Sue yelled. "This is my favorite show!"

He came closer to the camera. "I'm a former homicide detective, NYPD. *You* are surrounded by criminals. They're out there, and they're out to get *you*. And they. Are. Getting. Away. With it."

"Wooooo-hoooooo!" someone yelled. Catcalls erupted around the room.

CRIME OF THE CENTURY: THE GRIMSTONE HEIST.

Detective Shannon was now standing by a gray lake. "Ten years ago, on the night of a full moon, the peaceful community of Fortune Falls was invaded by a gang of thieves. Their target? The multimillion-dollar jewel collection of Carlotta Grimstone, one of the wealthiest women in the world."

"Fortune Falls?" Mandy Sue sat up straighter. "That's just a half-hour away. We're famous!"

Fortune Falls was also Alfie's hometown — where he was buried. March felt a prick of alertness, a sense that something was coming that he might not want to know.

A photograph flashed on the screen, and Jules gave March a quick, startled glance. It was the woman who had accosted them at the cemetery! He recognized the deep grooves around her mouth, the unnaturally plump lips, the black hair drawn straight back and tucked behind her ears.

Detective Shannon strolled toward the camera. "Carlotta inherited her wealth through the Grimstone family. You may have heard of them — Grimstone Tires, Grimstone Industries, and, of course, now the famous Grimstone Trust. Carlotta herself, at eighty, is still prominent in society life in Manhattan."

A shot of Carlotta in a red gown at some society bash.

"Granny is rocking that *tiara*!" one of the kids hooted.

"But that night, ten years ago, Carlotta was not at her lakefront summer home. Instead, three thieves were looting the house of her most precious possessions: her jewels. But these are not ordinary jewels."

A shot of Carlotta talking:

"Yes, I collect jewels that are cursed. I don't believe in curses. I believe in the *anticurse*, if you will. If I buy these stones and if I'm not afraid, I am gaining courage every day I own them." She smiled. "In my younger days, they called me Fate's Temptress."

Mike Shannon again. "That night, the thieves slipped in and out without tripping the alarm. Their prize? The twenty-five-million-dollar Makepeace Diamond. Cursed. The Crack in the Sky, the priceless turquoise stone rumored to have been responsible for the death and financial ruin of each of its owners. Catherine the Great's emerald brooch, smuggled out of Russia in the nineteenth century. But there was one theft that Carlotta Grimstone couldn't forgive."

Seven iridescent stones in a necklace flashed on the screen, worn around the scrawny neck of Carlotta.

"The Seven Sacred Moonstones," Mike Shannon said.

March flinched. Jules turned around and shook her head at him as if to say, *This is crazy.*

"Said to have been carved from Merlin's cave. Rumored to tell fortunes, predict fates . . . and foretell the future. Which makes them magic. And . . . priceless."

March's fingers itched to dig into his secret pocket. He thought of Carlotta Grimstone saying, *They are rough magic. Cruel. But real.*

"It was this last theft that destroyed Carlotta Grimstone."

A shot of Carlotta again, this time looking haggard.

"Carlotta believed in the legend. The moonstones were her protection against fate. Or so she believed. Who stole them? Police suspect the three most ruthless jewel thieves in the history of American criminals."

A face flashed on the screen. March smothered his gasp. It was Alfie.

21

HOW TO STEAL A FORTUNE

The photograph was an old one. Alfie looked younger, lean and handsome in a dinner jacket.

Thieves avoid being photographed. If March wanted a photo of his dad, he'd have to reach for a mug shot. Now here was his father's grin, his way of cocking his head slightly at you, as if he was inviting you in closer to hear something outrageous or to share a joke. March's face felt red with the effort to look unmoved. He sat very still.

"Alfred McQuin, aka Gentleman Alfie, successful jewel thief, second-story man, and con artist."

Jules stared straight at the TV, hugging her knees very hard.

"Was he working with this man?"

A mug shot of a handsome guy, smiling. Usually men in mug shots looked evil or unshaven or tired or pissed off, but this guy looked like a frat boy on a beach with a frozen margarita. Blond, blue eyed, and smug.

"Robert Oscar Ford grew up in Indiana. A farm boy, a basketball forward with a scholarship to Duke and a bright future. Instead he pulled off his first heist at seventeen, knocking over his fiancée's father's jewelry store. Then he disappeared. Within a few years he was on the FBI's most wanted list. That night, ten years ago, he was caught red-handed with Crack in the Sky, as well as the emerald brooch. Oscar Ford was put away for nine long years. He is currently out on parole."

A photo flashed on-screen, one March had never seen before. His mother was leaning back on a blanket in the grass, laughing.

She looked so young and pretty. Jules looked so much like her. If you took away the bad attitude and the scowl.

"As for the last suspect, this mysterious, beautiful brunette could be the key. Maggie Barnes was a student when she met Alfie McQuin. It was love at first sight, and rumor has it that it wasn't long after their hasty marriage that crafty McQuin lured young Maggie into being an accomplice on his jobs."

No! Alfie didn't lure *her! They loved each other!*

"The body of Maggie Barnes was found the day after the heist, washed up at the foot of Fortune Falls. Alfred McQuin disappeared.

"What happened that night? Why did Maggie Barnes tumble down the falls? Why did Alfred McQuin disappear? Did they see their dark fortunes? Was it too much to bear? We'll never know. Because only a month ago . . ." March closed his eyes as the headlines he remembered so well flashed on-screen.

". . . McQuin fell off a roof in Amsterdam in the middle of a heist, his pockets stuffed with diamonds. Oscar Ford was released from the penitentiary in April. If he knows anything about the missing jewels, he isn't talking." Shannon faced the screen, mist curling behind him. "What happened to the Makepeace Diamond? Are Merlin's magic moonstones lost forever?"

"McQuin," one of the kids said. "Hey, new kid, isn't that . . ."

Darius grabbed the remote from the table. "Hey, what

about the basketball play-offs?" he asked, and changed the channel.

Someone yelled that it wasn't fair, and Pete yelled for his remote back, and someone else shoved somebody, and Pete finally got the remote and snapped off the TV with a show of weary authority.

"Obviously we're having trouble with our behavior tonight."

"That's okay, Pete," Darius said. "We forgive you, bro."

"Television privileges are canceled. You all have Darius to thank."

Everyone groaned and stood up.

Jules looked stunned as she filed toward the door with Izzy. March pressed forward, trying to get near her. The girls headed down the corridor toward the back door.

Darius spoke from behind him. "That dude . . . the jewel thief. He's your pops, isn't he? How come you don't have diamonds on the soles of your shoes?"

"He didn't leave me any diamonds."

Jules turned. "He didn't leave us squat," she said.

"What about the magic moonstones?" March asked her. "What if that crazy Grimstone lady was right? What if Alfie still had them, and —"

"You're as crazy as she is!" Jules pinned him with her furious gaze. "Don't you get it? He was a jerk, a louse, a loser! He got our mother into stealing!"

"What does that guy know?" March sputtered. "He's just looking for ratings!"

"What do *you* know? When are you going to stop looking at your father as some kind of hero?"

"When you stop trashing him!"

Mandy Sue loomed up in the dim corridor. "What's going on here? No mixing with the girls, fellas. You know that."

"Hey, Mandy Sue, give us a break. For once," Darius said, disgust clear in his voice. "They were just talking."

"Tone!" Mandy Sue said brightly. "Sounded like arguing to me. And that's not allowed at Polestar, is it?" She shook her finger at March and Jules. "You should be role models for these two. After all, Izzy has tried again and again to mainstream with fosters, and . . ." She put a heavy hand on Izzy's shoulder. ". . . they always kick you back, don't they, sweetie? She's so . . . unwanted. And Darius . . . a mother in jail, a father who —"

"Shut up!" Darius shouted, taking a step toward her.

"Intimidation!" Mandy Sue shrilled. "Pete!"

Pete rushed down the hallway.

"Darius threatened me!" Mandy Sue cried.

"He did not," March said. "He just told you to shut up."

Pete grabbed Darius by the collar. "That's the last of your chances, Mr. Fray. We're sending you back to juvie! Let them deal with your attitude."

"You can't do that!" Izzy cried.

"Oh yes, I can." Pete pushed his face close to Izzy's. "Do you want to go back to the psych ward? Just say the word."

Izzy drifted near Darius. Both of their faces had gone completely blank. March wished he could do that, put the pain behind a mask. If he stayed here long enough, he knew he'd develop the skill. He'd have to. He'd be one of the walking wounded, like Darius and Izzy.

The future rushed at him with all its terror. He had to get out.

He thought of the two jokers, fitting together. He and Jules weren't the perfect fit. But Alfie had told him to find her, and he couldn't leave her.

I'd rather calculate the odds and take the risk than wait for fate to fall out of the sky.

He needed a plan.

March slept through the alarm and woke up only when Darius shook him. He floated up to consciousness and focused on his face.

"It's Jules, man," Darius said. "She ran away."

22

SO MUCH FOR SIBS

Well, so much for loyalty.

"Did she tell you where she was going?" Mandy Sue demanded. Her hands fluttered. "Everything happens to me. There'll be another investigation . . . All that paperwork! All those inspectors, asking questions . . ."

"Now calm down, Mandy Sue. That doesn't have to happen." Pete paced the floor of his office. "I'm sure March doesn't want his sister to get in trouble — do you, son?"

When they use the word son, *start worrying.*

"Nossir."

"Tell us about it. Did she run away?" Pete asked. He gave the appearance of someone barely containing himself from leaping across the room and grabbing March by the throat. "Tell us what you know!"

"I don't know anything!"

"Save it for someone who's stupid," Pete spit out.

"I thought I just did," March said.

It took several long moments for Pete to comprehend that he'd been insulted. He pointed a crooked index finger at March.

"You are a troublemaker," he said. "You're going to wind up just like your roommate!"

"Pete, what are we going to do?" Mandy Sue wailed.

"We're going to sit tight, that's what. Chances are the little lady will realize how good she has it here at Polestar, and she'll find her way home. We'll think of a story and whatnot, and we'll tell you, March, and you'll stick to it, you hear me? Answer me!"

"Sure. I'll stick to the script."

Pete leaned over and fixed his bloodshot gaze on March. "You better be telling the truth. I got my eye on you."

March was heading up to bed the next evening when he heard the TV blaring the news. He stopped in his tracks outside the den when he heard the word *heist*. A penthouse robbery on the Upper East Side of New York was baffling police. A diamond and sapphire necklace and a moonstone ring had been stolen from television reporter Michelle Westlake.

He stood watching the coverage, watching it the way Alfie would have watched it. For the details.

Security system was on. Motion sensors did not trip. Doors still locked in the morning. The only thing they found were two small holes drilled in the skylight. Lobby surveillance tapes were being studied. A new cleaning crew had been hired, but the superintendent didn't know anything about it.

March watched blurry surveillance photos of a cleaning crew moving through the lobby. He saw a tall man in a painter's cap who looked vaguely familiar. And a shorter fellow with a backpack vacuum who kept his face down and away from the camera. He rubbed his knuckle against his lip.

Every sensor in March's brain lit up.

It wasn't a *he*. It was Jules.

23

THIS HEIST SUCKS

How could he be sure?

He just was.

Jules . . . with all her talk about Alfie, *she* was the biggest liar ever.

March took the stairs two at a time. He burst into the room. Darius was shoving things in a duffel.

"I'm out of here tomorrow, Marco," he said. "Bounced." He looked up and caught March's expression. "Don't get all emo on me, bro. You got to learn not to make attachments."

March was breathing hard. He crossed the room to his backpack and took out Alfie's list. He spread it on the desk.

"I found Jules," he said.

"Good. She okay?"

1. PARTICLE ZOO
2. ROOM SERVICE
3. VACUUM PACKED
4-5. SURFING MURPH
6. WET PAINT
7. PLASTIC REPLICA

"Seems like it. She just pulled off a major jewel heist."

"Yeah. And tomorrow I'm heading to Harvard. Early admission."

March leaned against the desk. "I didn't go to school

much. I went to Alfie McQuin's Homeschool for Thieves instead. He taught me about cons and heists. How a heist could be the most perfect con ever. How details matter. He had favorite heists of all time, and I just figured out that this" — and he slammed his finger on the paper — "is a list of them. Number three? Vacuum packed? That's how the heist last night was done."

"What heist?" Darius said. "You mean that television reporter? Are you saying that your sister, Jules . . . stole her *jewels*?"

March nodded. "And I think she did it with Oscar Ford, the guy on TV the other night."

Darius leaned backward. "I gotta sit down."

"Jules used a vacuum cleaner — an industrial one, the kind you wear on your back, and I'm guessing it had a boosted engine. They got in as cleaners, and she stayed behind — probably hid in an AC duct. Meanwhile Oscar goes up to the roof and drills two holes in the skylight. Later that night he drops down the sling from there — the kind of thing Jules used in her act. She gets out, winds herself into the sling, and hangs *over* the jewelry. She sucks up the necklace with the vacuum. Then she hides in the duct again, and Oscar pulls up the sling. She gets out the next day before the theft was discovered, but after the security system is turned off. Nobody checks their valuables before they turn off the system. Probably the maid comes in, inputs the code, gets the coffee going, or whatever. Jules waits for her chance and splits."

"That's a *movie*," Darius said. "My dad was a Hollywood producer, and he would have snapped that stuff up."

March tapped the paper again. "It's happened before, just in a different way. There were these famous heists in France that really made Alfie laugh. At this supermarket chain. How the money was handled was like this — a tube would suck it from the registers right into the safe. So the thieves broke in, and they cut into the tube, stuck in a modified vacuum hose, and just sucked the money out of the safe. They pulled off a whole bunch of heists doing that."

"They vacuumed up money? Sweet!" Darius shook his head. "Does that mean your old man was planning on doing it?"

"I think so, yeah," March said. "He knew his way around an AC duct."

"So how did Oscar know about it?"

"The only thing I can guess is that Jules already knew Oscar. He gets out of prison and finds out my dad is planning some heists. He wants in on the action. He recruits Jules. She was conning me the whole time — biding her time. Alfie used to say that ninety percent of a successful heist is planning. He figured out the method. Jules found the list, memorized it, and told Oscar. She could have done it on the plane — snooped while I was sleeping."

"That's some nasty double cross," Darius said. "You two are related. You just don't do that to family. I mean, *my* family, yeah. You can't trust *anybody*."

March felt a dark tide of rage move through him. His hands shook. Sure, they weren't close. But he wouldn't have left without her. He would have watched out for her, just like Alfie had wanted him to. "Well, she did it to me."

Izzy suddenly slid out from underneath Darius's bed. "Welcome to the club," she said, her dark eyes full of sadness. "Family stinks."

24

THE BEST PLANS ARE CRAZY

"Iz here just sneaked in to see me," Darius said. "We've been taking care of each other for three years now. Don't want to stop. She was going to see if she could fit in my duffel. Crazy plan, right?"

"The best plans are crazy," March said.

Izzy peered at the list. "So your dad made a list of heists he wanted to do, and the way to do them. But how do you know the targets?"

"That's the piece that's missing," March said. "I think the answer is here." He spilled out the contents of his backpack onto the desk. "Here's what he left me. A book, a key, a deck of marked cards. Whatever the missing piece is, I think Jules figured it out."

He looked at the list again, thinking hard.

"The heist in Amsterdam was number two — Room Service. I know that for sure. Alfie lifted a waiter uniform from the hotel basement. That's how he got access to the hallways. It only works in big hotels, and you've got to be careful, because there's managers everywhere, and even in big hotels everybody knows everybody. But one of Alfie's rules is: *There's always a new guy.*"

"So he got into the room that way?"

"Not the room, the room above. It was empty. He reserved it for a late check-in but he didn't show up, because then you have to give your passport and ID. He was supposed to rappel down from that balcony, spring the lock on the door, enter, snatch the diamonds, and get out. The target was a jewelry dealer. It all went fine except, for some reason, instead of using the drainpipe to get down, he went up to the roof. I still don't know why. And that's when . . ."

He suddenly couldn't say the words *he fell.*

Darius shook out the deck of cards. "These aren't marked cards."

"Some of them have numbers on them," March pointed out.

Darius shook his head. "That's not how you mark a deck. You crease a card with your fingernail or bend it. What kind of a criminal's kid *are* you?"

"If your dad was leaving you clues, he'd leave you easy ones," Izzy said. "He'd have to be sure that you'd get it." She looked over Darius's shoulder as he pulled out the cards with numbers on the backs.

"Look," she said, putting them in order. "The cards are all diamonds — 2, 3, 4, 5, 6, and 7. Maybe he's directing you back to the list."

"Or a straight flush," Darius noted.

"The numbers on the 2 card are 104 / 11 1 1 2 5 24 14 28 2 6 20 54 3 26 8 14 2 3 13 13."

"Computer code?" Darius asked.

"Are you a coder?" Izzy asked March.

He shook his head. "I can log in and log out, but . . ."

"A Swiss bank account?" Darius asked.

"Possibly . . ." Izzy said. "But why would there be different numbers for each card? Wouldn't six Swiss bank accounts be overkill?"

"Not if there were huge piles of cash and jewels," Darius pointed out hopefully.

Izzy's gaze lighted on *The Moonstone*. "Was your dad a big reader?"

March shook his head. "Newspapers and magazines and detective stuff."

Izzy picked up the book. "This is considered to be the first detective novel ever written."

"How do you know these things?" Darius asked.

"I read," she said distractedly.

She turned to a page. "Do you have a pencil and paper?" she asked. "This could be a book code."

Darius looked at March. They both shrugged. "Best to let her fly," Darius said.

Glancing from the playing card to the book, Izzy began writing down letters.

HEINMULDER

She pushed the paper toward March.

He let out a breath. "Hein Mulder was the mark. The jewelry dealer in Amsterdam. How did you do that?"

"The first number — 104 — is the page number. Then notice the spacing? The first number is the line, the second number is the space. So, I counted eleven lines down, and the first space was the letter *H* in the word *he*. And so on. If we go through the numbers on these cards, we'll get the rest of your dad's targets."

"She's a genius," Darius said. "Have I mentioned that?"

"The weird thing is that there's nothing on the aces," Izzy said. "So there's no way to know who the target is for the first heist."

"Let's just keep going," March said.

It took a while, but soon they had a list of names.

MICHELLEWESTLAKE

DOLORESLEON

BLANCHEPOTTAGE
RENEEROOTER

"Michelle Westlake is the TV reporter who got ripped off yesterday!" March said. "She goes with *Vacuum Packed.* So Dolores Leon must go with *Surfing Murph.*"

"Any clue what *Surfing Murph* means?" Darius asked.

"Sure. Easy one," March said. "Murph the Surf was the nickname the press gave the guy who pulled off a heist at the Museum of Natural History in New York City back in the sixties. They got in through a bathroom window and stole the Star of India, this really famous star sapphire."

"So if we plop Dolores Leon and Museum of Natural History into a search engine, we might get some kind of match," Izzy said. "We can look it up on Pete's computer."

"How? It's almost lights-out."

"He's always snoring by eleven. Just leave the back door open for me. I'll be back."

At midnight the house was dark and quiet. Pete's office was locked, but it took less than a minute for March to break in.

Izzy's slight fingers flew on the keys. "Dolores Leon, Museum of Natural History . . . Whoa. She's donating her famous necklace, the Widow's Knot, to the museum's *Gem Folklore* exhibition — like, famous jewelry pieces that have a story behind them. They're throwing a big fancy party at the museum to honor her."

"What's the Widow's Knot?" March asked.

"It's an amber gemstone with a clasp of two moonstones. You think Jules is going to try to steal this next, ha-ha?" Izzy mimicked Mandy Sue's fake laugh.

"Moonstones again," March murmured.

"Like the show?" Darius asked. "The magic moonstones your pop stole?"

"My dad didn't believe in magic," March said. "He believed in cash."

"Word," Darius said.

March felt something stir inside him, some small flame that kicked into life and became a blaze of certainty. He leaned over Izzy's shoulder and studied the necklace. This collection of stones and metal was his ticket out. He could feel it. That's what Alfie would want. His father would've been devastated thinking about March in a place that smelled like cherry mouthwash and "nobody cares." He'd want him to grab his fate and make it dance. That's why he wrote down the heists. March knew it now. Alfie never wrote down anything; it was all in his head. He'd left him a message, and it was *find the stones.*

"I'm going to steal it," he said.

"Yeah, right." Darius reared back. "You're serious? That's crazy."

March nodded. "For sure. And you two would have to be crazy to join me."

Darius and Izzy exchanged a glance.

"Just . . . go?" Izzy looked uncertain.

"Leave all this?" Darius asked, with a sardonic twist to his mouth.

"What have you got to lose?" March asked. One corner of his mouth quirked upward. "Creamed corn?"

25

SO LONG, DUMPSVILLE

They waited for first light, and they ran all the way to the station. The grass smelled sweet and damp. The moon was still hanging on, not giving up on nighttime, even though pink was streaking through the stacked clouds in a sky so charged with dark, luminous blue it seemed electric. They ran, laughing at nothing except the fact that they were running, flying down blacktop roads, past the dark windows, gulping down morning air.

They swung onto the train with a few sleepy commuters. They paid for their tickets with the cash they'd pooled and crashed back against the seats, exhilarated at the sight of the miles put between them and Polestar House.

Izzy stared out the window, wide-eyed. "It's such a big world. I forgot."

"That's a good thing," Darius said. He leaned back against the seat. "How much is a yacht? I think I'd like to buy a yacht for me and you. We'll sail away."

Izzy leaned her head against him. In just minutes, she was asleep.

"You and Izzy?" March asked. "You're . . ."

"Girls aren't my thing, Marco. She's like my little sister," Darius said. He looked down at Izzy. "She looks like she's ten or something, but she's thirteen. Her parents didn't pay much attention to her. Hackers with gambling issues. They decide to take a trip to Atlantic City, and they lock her in the apartment while they're gone. They leave her with enough food for two days and they're gone for five. She was four years old. They took her away then. She saw them on supervised visits for a while. Then they stopped showing up. She hates small spaces. Wound up in a hospital once when a foster family locked her in a closet. That's why I watch out for her. My dad was in the secret service. She knows I can protect her, I've got it in my genes."

Darius yawned. "Gotta catch some winks. When I wake up, point me the way to Easy Street."

Within seconds Darius was snoring lightly. March watched town after town go by, a sense of dread beginning to build inside him. He'd been so cocky! They needed a place to sleep, a place to plan the heist. Between the three of them, they had only about thirty dollars. They needed more. Money for food, for better clothes, for equipment. They needed cell phones. Alfie had given him a direction, not a plan.

They needed a warm-up con.

He gripped the I LOVE NY key chain. What had Alfie left him? Could there be a place in New York somewhere, a place Alfie would call a bolt hole, somewhere already set up for a hideout, a small apartment in a boring neighborhood where no one would notice them?

Alfie must have bought the key chain at Grand Central Terminal. There was a picture of the grand columned building on the other side of the I LOVE NY logo. He worried it between his thumb and index finger in anxiety. He felt something pop. He'd broken it.

Sighing, March studied the cheap key chain. It hadn't taken much to break it.

Not much at all . . .

He worked his fingernail into the gap, and it split open. Inside was a small folded piece of paper. He unwrapped it. Written in Alfie's handwriting was:

TRACK 61.

26

TRACK 61

They stood in the enormous waiting room, beneath the clicking schedule board that supplied its heartbeat. Commuters rushed by them, juggling briefcases and bags of bagels.

"There is no track sixty-one," Darius said.

"Yes, there is," Izzy said. "It's an abandoned track that was used by President Franklin D. Roosevelt. He was in a wheelchair, so they'd drive his car straight out of the train and onto an elevator that went right up into the Waldorf Astoria Hotel."

She held up a smart phone. "I looked it up on secretivecity.com." She saw March's expression when he saw the phone. "I found it on the train. People really need to watch their stuff."

"I should mention that Izzy has certain . . . talents," Darius said. "We met when I found her hand in my pocket."

"We'd better ditch it," March advised. "It has a tracker on it."

"It's okay. I already know the way to the platform."

Izzy didn't break stride as she dropped the phone on the counter by the information booth. She continued into a corridor and led them to an unmarked brass door. She handed March a paper clip. "Your turn."

Darius and Izzy stood in front of March as he worked the lock. He pushed the door open, and they slipped inside.

A narrow stairway led straight down. They followed it as the bustle and noise of the station above decreased and the sound of a train entering the station thundered through the soles of their shoes. A shiver ran down March's spine. For the first time since leaving Amsterdam, he felt close to his pop, as though Alfie were right next to him on the stairs.

They came out onto an unused train platform scattered with debris. One light in a cage sputtered overhead. An old Coke bottle lay furred with dust. They picked their way through construction equipment, piles of trash, and orange plastic netting. Across the dark expanse of columns and tracks, they could make out the other platforms. A train had just arrived and people poured out of the doors, hurrying down the platform toward the exit.

No one noticed them. It was like being a ghost, a spectral presence in the busy station.

A rusted dark blue car sat nearby on unused tracks. They picked their way across the flung railroad ties and bits of metal and trash. March tripped his way up the stair that led to the door. He hesitated, then pushed it open. Instead of the passenger seats he'd been expecting, the car was empty.

He felt the thud of disappointment. What had he been expecting? A box full of answers with a bow on top? He kicked an empty can across the floor.

You led me here. Now talk to me, Pop.

March opened the electrical panel box. "There isn't anything," he said. Disappointment rang through him, heavy and dull.

"If your pops left you something, it was probably lifted already," Darius said. "Street folks tend to take anything that isn't nailed down." He waved at the graffiti outside the dusty window. "It's not like we're the first people to find this place. Look at all these taggers."

March rotated in frustration. Alfie wasn't stupid. There was something here. Something he was meant to find.

Outside the car, graffiti splashed the walls, puffy letters announcing *I was here* to an indifferent world.

If he stood still and looked straight out the front of the car, he could see it. Centered in his sightline, outlined in black, red letters three feet high:

MATT HENNEBERRY COME HOME

March felt the hairs on his neck tingle. "We're in the right place," he said.

27

FINDING A PIGEON

They stood on the abandoned track, staring at the graffiti. The Matt Henneberry tag was isolated from the others, except for DOMINICK PH next to it.

"Matt Henneberry was an alias we used sometimes," March said. "Alfie thought it was the friendliest name in the world."

"Who's Dominick?" Izzy asked.

"It must be someone else," March said. "Alfie never used that name." He blinked hard. "I thought he didn't leave me a message. Just random weird stuff. But he *did* leave me this."

"What does it mean?" Izzy asked.

"I don't know." The exhilaration was wearing off. Alfie had left him a message that he couldn't read. Again. March closed his fist around the key in his pocket. *Come home.*

Where, Alfie? Where is home?

He stared until his eyes were burning. Izzy and Darius were quiet. Finally Darius's hand landed on his shoulder. It was enough to buckle his knees.

"It's okay, bro. You'll figure it out. Time to get moving."

Yes. He should get moving. A train roared into a platform nearby. People coming, people going, all around them. They needed a direction, too.

Figure out what you have. Figure out what you need. Then use what you have to get what you need.

He had a custom-made jacket with British tailoring.

He needed cash.

"I have a plan," March said. "It's time for a pigeon drop."

The students at the Huntington–Chumley School wore uniforms. March remembered this from his time in New York with Alfie. They'd run a job that required March to look like a fancy private-school kid, so Alfie had taken him to the Farquar-Mooney Thrift Shop, and they'd purchased a navy blazer. March had worn it to a dinner with Alfie and a former South American military dictator. A month later the dictator had discovered his secret offshore account had been drained.

That job had financed a lease on a house in the Scottish countryside. That had been a good year, until Alfie had been tempted to lift a Chagall painting from some earl's wall and they had to leave the country quickly. . . .

Don't be an owl. Don't look back.

It was time for school when they reached the Huntington–Chumley campus. Mothers and nannies were heading to the school, the mothers wearing skinny pants and sky-high heels and carrying purses made of leather so soft and supple it looked like candy. The nannies wore cardigans and loafers and pushed strollers with the younger siblings of the elite students.

"They're gonna rule the world one day," Darius said. "Hurl."

March lounged against the brick wall across the street, his eyes moving.

"What are we looking for?" Darius asked.

"Patterns. Habit is our best friend. Watch who walks in with the kid, who doesn't. Who's a nanny, who's a mom. Who chats with the other moms, who doesn't. We have to pick our pigeon. We'll run the con tomorrow. We don't have time for a second chance. This is Wednesday. The party is Friday night."

Across the street, a black Mercedes sedan drew up. A uniformed driver got out and walked a small girl, maybe five years old, into the building, holding her hand. March glanced at his watch.

He shifted his attention to a woman walking with a young boy, maybe eight or nine. She was dressed the same as the other women, but just a bit . . . more. Her purse was bright pink, not the discreet shades of the others'. Her heels were higher, her bracelets thicker, her hair too blond. He watched as she said hello to the other moms, and how they responded with tight smiles and turned away.

Meanwhile the uniformed driver came out, saluted a teacher standing on the stairs, and headed for his car. As he drove off, a Range Rover pulled up. A kid got out and ran into the building. The too-blond mom waved at the Range Rover driver but looked crestfallen when the car just zoomed away. Her kid gave up trying to say good-bye to her and walked into school.

"The pigeon drop is an old con, but it still works," March said. "The trick is to mix it up with new details. The basic con is this — you drop a bag of money on the sidewalk, then wait for a mark to come. You pick it up. You say, 'Wow, look at all this money. What should we do?' And you work it out eventually that the mark gives you his wallet while he takes the bag and stuffs it in his pocket or down his pants or whatever. And then he walks off thinking he made a cool five thousand. Only he's got a bag full of paper and you've got his wallet."

"What kind of pigeon would fall for that?" Darius asked.

"Insecure, needy social climber," March said. He pointed to the too-blond woman with his chin. "That one."

28

THE PIGEON DROP

SHOPPING LIST:
WHITE SHIRT, STRIPED TIE, GRAY FLANNEL PANTS
MINIATURE LIECHTENSTEIN FLAGS
KNOCKOFF DESIGNER BRIEFCASE
SILLY PUTTY

"Alfie had a saying," March told Darius and Izzy as he nervously fiddled with his tie the next morning. "'Find what they're hungry for.' Our pigeon wants social status. She's not just walking her kid to school; she's looking to make a *connection* with these rich folks."

"The kid was beside the point," Izzy said. "She hardly paid attention to him."

"Exactly. Those other moms are dissing her every single day, and she knows it. She's got money, but she doesn't belong. We're going to dangle what she wants in front of her. If all goes well, we'll walk away with at least a grand. And she'll have a good story."

"How do you know?" Izzy asked, biting her lip.

"I don't," March said. "When you run a con, you don't think about the odds. You think about details so you don't mess up. Alfie always said, 'If you're going to do something, don't do it stupid.' We just have to stay cool and stay smart. Ready?"

"Yeah," Darius said. "But why do I have to be the bad guy?"

"Because you look scary," Izzy said.

"I do not."

"Do, too."

"Guys? Can we keep our eye on the con?"

At 8:23 a.m., the woman with the pink purse walked down the street with her son. Again, she nodded at the other mothers, who offered brief, chilly smiles.

The Mercedes pulled up. The driver got out, came around to the other side, and opened the door. The little girl got out, and they walked toward the school.

Izzy hurried down the street. March watched as she slapped the Silly Putty on each side of the car's front hood and stuck the Liechtenstein flags in.

March crossed the street and stood by the car. He dropped the fake designer briefcase they'd purchased from a street vendor downtown.

Pink-purse woman said good-bye to her son, who walked up the stairs.

Darius suddenly loped around her, startling her. She clutched her purse closer. He ran past and snatched up March's briefcase, then dashed down the block.

"Oh no!" March cried in an accent Alfie called fake Romanian, because it was attached to no particular country. *"Stoppen den dieb!"*

With one glance the woman took in the diplomatic flags and March in the blue blazer. She tottered over in her heels. "I saw that . . . street person," she said. "He almost stole my purse! Are you all right?" She looked around. "We should tell security. . . ."

"No, vait," March said. "They said back in Vaduz that New York is dangerous, but I . . . oh!" He clapped his hands to his mouth. "I hope . . . I didn't . . ." He searched in his chest pocket. "Oh, I still have it." He took out the check that the gang had fabricated and worked over at a copy shop. "For the school trip to ze supercollider." He held out the check so that it was clearly visible.

The woman's eyes widened as she took in BANK OF LIECHTENSTEIN and the royal seal. The check was made out to the Huntington–Chumley School and was in the amount of $10,000.

"Ah, you're from . . ."

"Liechtenstein, yes. My papa is the new ambassador . . . and he vas to come with me today to pay for ze trip. But he receives a call and he's off to our plane to fly for a meeting in Washington. . . ."

"Yes, that must happen often. . . ."

"And entrusts me with the check. If it had been stolen . . . jail for me, I think! Heh! Instead ze criminal boy steals my new Vuitton satchel!"

"Perhaps I could . . . talk to your mother for you."

"The baroness?"

"She's . . ." The woman gulped. ". . . a baroness? Let me call her for you on my phone. You seem upset."

"No, she is . . . swimming her laps right now," March said. "But I will tell her about your kindness, and you should come to the embassy for tea."

The woman beamed. "Oh, I'd love that." She stuck out her hand. "Virginia Hayes."

"Gerhard Richter," March said. Then he looked at the check again. "Oh *nein*! Ze . . . ze check isn't signed! And today is the last day for the trip!"

"Oh, but I'm sure that the school . . . being who your father is . . . there's leeway. . . ."

March's eyes filled with tears. "It is the last day. *Mein*

Vater won't forgive this. Even though it was him who forgets to sign the check! Do I have time to get to the embassy before the day begins?" He looked around wildly.

"Dear, you must calm down," Virginia Hayes said. "I think I can help you. My bank is right on that corner. Why don't I give you some money right now? I can't do ten thousand dollars, of course, but surely a portion for a deposit would hold your place. . . ."

"Oh, I could not ask. . . ."

"You didn't ask, dear. I offered."

"Well . . . maybe a thousand?" March wiped his eyes. "But I couldn't. . . ."

"Come with me," she said firmly. "We wouldn't want you to get the wrong impression about America. Not after that horrible, grimy street person stole your lovely Vuitton bag."

March swung into step beside her. "My mother shall call you for tea at the embassy. She will serve you our famous *gesundenheitenflachen*!"

29

CASING THE JOINT

March went through every bathroom in the Museum of Natural History. Since Murph the Surf's day, security had improved, to say the least. He could see no way in. What was Alfie thinking?

You wanted me to pull off this heist, Pop. Give me a hint, will you?

Thanks to Virginia Hayes, the three of them had shopped at the computer store and now had smart phones and a tablet. He texted Darius.

no luck here. where r u

under the whale

He made his way to the Milstein Hall of Ocean Life. The hall was an enormous room with two levels of dioramas of fish and marine life. Hanging overhead was a model of a gigantic blue whale. This was the hall where the gala party would take place on Friday night. Tomorrow night.

He joined Darius and Izzy on the lower level, staring up at the whale.

"Ninety-four feet long, twenty-one thousand pounds, and made of fiberglass," Darius said.

"Adorable," March said. "So, for the event, this whole space will be filled with tables." He frowned. "Less than ideal conditions for a smash and grab."

March strolled the perimeter. Guards, cameras, unmarked doors with signs that said EMERGENCY EXIT ALARM WILL SOUND or NO ADMITTANCE.

The best way out would be on the lower level — *always avoid stairs if you can.* But he couldn't see weaving in and out of tables with an amber necklace in his hands.

"Any ideas?" Darius asked.

"As Alfie used to say, 'The getaway is always the biggest problem.' I'm worried about getting *in*, sure, but I'm mostly worried about getting *out*. There's security everywhere, and that's just the stuff I can *see*. There are always backup systems in place."

"Maybe Alfie didn't mean it literally," Darius said. "Like, what's the lesson of the original job? What did your pop admire about it?"

"Simplicity," March said. "Visit the place, open a window, come back later. But that was back in 1964. We've got alarms and guards. . . ."

"And people that night. And waiters, right?"

"And a stage," Izzy said.

March swiveled and regarded her. "What?"

She seemed to shrink under the attention. "For the choral concert," she said in a tiny voice. "Leon is a big benefactor of school choruses in New York City. They're picking the best ones of all the private schools, and they're all going to sing at the beginning of the evening."

March sprang forward and enveloped Izzy in a hug. She turned rosy. "I did good?"

"What are you thinking?" Darius asked.

March smiled.

30

NERVES

March felt perspiration trickle under his collar. He kept his restless hands in his pockets. If he showed nerves, Darius and Izzy would lose theirs.

They stood across the street from the museum. They were now all wearing blue blazers and gray flannels. They had bought a comb and used it. They had gone over the plan. Now all they had to do was wait.

How had Alfie done it? There had been many times when March waited in a hotel room while Alfie put on his dark clothes and went out on a job. March could sense his complete concentration, but not his nerves. How had Alfie controlled his own jumping skin, the thoughts crowding his brain about the million things that could go wrong?

Across the street the museum sprawled for blocks, massive gray stone, with a grand entrance, tall columns, waving banners. Police barricades had been set up, and bored photographers stood behind them, checking their equipment. A red carpet ran from the sidewalk all the way up the grand steps.

Suddenly their plan seemed impossible, crazy, foolish . . . destined to brand them *incorrigible* and land them in juvenile hall.

March saw Darius swallow. "You sure about this, Marco?"

"I'm sure," he said. Inside his pockets, he crossed his fingers. "Here's what we've got going for us. Nobody pays attention to kids. The security guys will be worried about the fancy folks. The fancy folks will be worried about looking good for each other. The museum people will be worried about the food and the drinks and that everything runs smoothly. All we have to do is steal the necklace."

"Right," Darius said. "That's all."

"After that, they'll want to get the chorus kids out as soon as possible so they can find the thief. I'll just walk out with it in my pocket. Easy peasy."

"Right," Darius said. "Except for the part where we steal the necklace. That's hard."

"Sure," March said. "Or we could go back to Polestar and eat creamed corn."

There was a short silence.

"Still in?" March asked.

"Still in."

31

MAXIMUM CHAOS

Lights winked on as twilight deepened. Floodlights illuminated the grand façade of the museum. The first limousine arrived, and a couple in formal wear headed up the wide stairs. Flashbulbs popped for a second, then stopped. The woman in the flowered gown dropped her fake smile and looked disappointed.

March kept his eyes on the photographers. That would be one way for Oscar Ford to sneak in. Or he and Jules could have already hidden themselves somewhere in the museum. Jules could be inside right now, her nerves pulled as taut as his.

He touched the moonstone in his pocket. It made him feel closer to Alfie. If only you could absorb steel-trap nerves and cool daring through a rock.

The limousines were now a long line of waiting cars. March nudged Darius as a yellow school bus pulled up and a bunch of kids spilled out, dressed in black pants and white shirts.

"Them?" Darius asked.

Wait for the moment of maximum chaos.

"Not yet," March said. "Five choral groups are coming. Somebody is always late. The later we go, the more pressure the people who run this thing are under. That's when things get overlooked."

The trickle of partygoers turned into a full-blast faucet of tuxedos and bright spring gowns. Skinny, long-necked women teetered out of limousines, posed, and slowly ascended the steps.

One choral group after another arrived. March counted them off on his fingers. A red-haired woman in a yellow-and-pink gown emerged from a limousine. She faced the photographers for long moments, allowing them to take hundreds of shots in an explosion of light and shutter noise. Something big gleamed from the neckline of her dress.

"Dolores Leon," Izzy said.

"And her necklace," March said.

A few straggling partygoers hurried from limousines. A black van made an illegal U-turn and bumped to a halt just a few feet from where they stood waiting. A nervous-looking woman jumped out and shouted, "Come on, get a move on, we're late!"

"This is us," March said. His mouth felt dry.

Students tumbled out of the van. The woman danced alongside the group, hurrying them forward.

March looked at Darius and Izzy. Darius's gaze was glassy with fear. "Now or never," March said.

Darius gave a quick glance at Izzy. She nodded.

"Go," they whispered together.

March ran forward and jogged alongside the frantic woman. "You late, too? We're from Huntington–Chumley."

"Bedford Prep. Traffic!" she panted.

Darius and Izzy dashed forward and attached themselves to the group as they ran toward a side door. An anxious young woman in a black dress peered out at them.

"Bedford Prep," the woman said, breathing hard.

"You are super late," the young woman said, frowning.

"Traffic!"

"They're starting in ten minutes. Follow me!"

And just like that, they were in.

March and Darius and Izzy followed the group down a dingy corridor and through the winding back corridors of the museum. They slipped into Milstein Hall from a back door marked NO ADMITTANCE. March made a note of where it was and saw that you didn't need a key. Waiters were using it to run food to the tables.

"Stand on the risers," the young woman whispered, even though the noise from the crowd was a steady, loud buzz. "The museum director will introduce you. You'll sing your number, and then remain on the stage while your benefactor, Mrs. Leon, presents the necklace and the director makes a short speech. After that the lights will go down, entrées will be served, and you'll exit out the same door."

March joined the others on the risers. He scanned the crowd anxiously. He looked carefully at each waiter and waitress. No sign of Oscar or Jules. That would be the easiest way to get close to Dolores Leon, he supposed, though he wondered how Jules could pass for a server. She looked older than twelve, but not that much older.

"This might be a good time to mention I can't sing," Darius whispered.

"Just mouth the words," March said.

"But what are we singing?"

"I hate this," Izzy said.

The director of the museum went to the microphone. She welcomed the crowd and went through a list full of people to thank. The crowd applauded politely.

March's gaze roamed the crowd. If Jules was out there, what was she thinking?

Alfie suddenly loomed in his head, his hand fluttering, saying, *Find Jules.* How would his old man feel if he knew his kids were now enemies, pitted against each other?

March pushed the uncomfortable thought away. Jules had been the one to take off. She'd started this.

And he was going to win it.

32

THE WIDOW'S KNOT

The director introduced Dolores Leon. The big necklace gleamed under the lights.

"And, now, thanks to the generosity of Mrs. Leon, so many schoolchildren in New York have found their voices. In her honor, they will sing her favorite song, 'My Heart Belongs to Daddy.' "

The choral director stood in front of them. He raised his hands, and then brought them down. Exactly on cue, all the voices sang out. Except for three.

March kept his gaze on Dolores Leon, who was standing off to the side, dabbing at her eyes with a handkerchief while she watched the singers.

When she turned her head, he studied the intricate clasp. Impossible to undo it quickly. Had to wait until she removed it herself.

Da-da dad, da da dad dad a dad . . .

March kept his mouth moving, but he didn't know the words. Most people in the crowd were smiling, some of them swaying a bit with the tune.

"Hey, we're rock stars!" Darius said to him under his breath.

The last note faded. Dolores Leon wiped away her last tear.

She approached the microphone. "Thank you, children. That was beautiful. I'm so touched. When children raise their voices in song, we hear the angels, don't we? Children are my passion. Children . . . and jewels."

She paused for the laughter. March noticed two security guards move closer.

"And to have both of my passions come together in one evening makes for a beautiful experience. Tonight I'm loaning my favorite necklace, the Widow's Knot, to the museum's *Gem Folklore* exhibition." She reached up to unclasp the necklace.

The director moved forward, smiling, to help her.

Dolores Leon held out the necklace, glittering in the white spotlight.

Izzy fainted.

"Give her some air!" Darius shouted.

March dropped through the risers and scrambled as fast as he could through the maze of feet. Before he could reach Dolores Leon, the spotlight moved, and he peered through the steps and followed the light . . . up, up to the shadowy heights of the ceiling.

High above them, a girl sat on top of the whale.

She wore a spangled mask and was dressed all in black. She stood on the whale's back, and the room went silent. Everyone stared at the tiny figure on the giant blue whale over their heads.

Jules.

She leaped off the whale, straight in midair. A collective gasp sucked the air out of the room. She had what looked like two silk ribbons in her hands. March knew they were strong and flexible.

He saw out of the corner of his eye that the director was confused. Dolores Leon was looking up, smiling, as though this were a delightful gift. The rest of the crowd thought it was part of a prearranged show, and they burst into applause as Jules landed in the swing created by the two pieces of fabric, then executed a dizzying spin. Little white lights were twined through her costume and in her hair.

The lights went out.

All anyone could see was the whirling lights overhead as Jules spun.

Distraction is the first rule of an open-air grab.

This was it — this was the strike! Heart pounding, March rolled out the end of the risers and ran toward Dolores Leon. He had to get there before Oscar.

A third security guard appeared. He slipped a pair of glasses out of his pocket and put them on. Infrared lenses. It was Oscar Ford, and he was moving fast.

March threw himself forward at Dolores. He muttered an apology, pretending to trip, and reached for the hand holding the necklace. It was empty!

Jules couldn't have swiped it, she was still up there. He could see the spinning lights. And Oscar was still a few paces away.

Distraction . . .

March looked closer. Jules hadn't been twirling at all. There was no one on the swing.

"My necklace is GONE!" Dolores screamed.

Jules had stolen the necklace right out from under him!

"TURN ON THE LIGHTS!" the director yelled into the microphone.

March looked around frantically. He saw a slender column of light as the door marked NO ADMITTANCE was cracked.

"CLOSE THE EXITS!" the director shouted, but her voice was lost in the noise of the crowd.

March leaped off the stage and charged toward the door after Jules.

33

TEDDY AND THE DOLLY

He dashed down the hallway. As he rounded the corner, he saw her disappear through another door.

"Check the exits!" someone shouted.

March dived through the door after Jules. He found himself in a dark gallery, facing a couple of musk oxen on a snowy hill. He stifled a shout of surprise.

Across the hall, two moose were fighting. One was goring the other with enormous antlers.

Heart slamming, he stopped and listened for the sound of footsteps. He heard light footfalls coming from the darkness. Cautiously he began to jog toward the sound.

Gazelles and wildebeests stared at him with glassy serenity as he ran past. He reached the end of the hall. Jules was nowhere in sight.

Izzy and Darius ran up, breathing hard. "Security is fanning out," Darius said. "And Oscar is right on our heels. He saw you jump off the platform. Do you have the necklace?"

"Jules has it!"

"Then just forget about it! I heard one of them say they're going to set up checkpoints. We've got to get out of here."

March wanted to stamp his foot in frustration. He'd bungled the job.

But Darius was right. They had to get away clean.

"There's an exit this way," he said.

They raced out into an anteroom near an exit of the museum. The round room was deserted except for a bronze statue of Teddy Roosevelt seated on a bench. Pushed against the wall were folded-up extra tables and a dolly — basically a rough board on wheels. The exit doors were locked and bolted. They probably had only seconds.

Running full tilt, Jules burst into the space.

For a moment they just looked at each other.

"You can't get away from us," March said.

"I'm trying to get away from Oscar, you idiot," Jules panted. "Help me push this thing." She ran to the dolly and pushed it closer to the bench with the statue. Then she stood behind the former president. "Come *on*!" she urged. "Help me!"

"Are you crazy? It's too heavy!"

"If you keep standing there, it sure is. Help me tip it onto the dolly. This is the only door that's not guarded."

The three ran over. They put their shoulders and hands on the statue.

"One, two, *three*!"

Teddy rocked, but did not tip.

"One more time," Jules said. "Come on, Darius, you're the one with the muscles! One, two, *three*!"

Slowly, Teddy Roosevelt toppled onto the dolly. His nose smashed against the board, his butt in the air.

"Push!" Jules urged.

A meaty hand landed on the back of March's shirt.

"Hand it over, kid," Oscar snarled. "You're out of your league."

Oscar spun him around and took a fistful of his shirt near his collar. Buttons popped as he bunched it in his hand and twisted it. March felt a sudden inability to breathe.

"The rest of security is heading this way. I want the necklace." He twisted the material tighter. March felt his airway closing. Black spots appeared in front of his eyes.

Jules spoke quietly. "Oscar, let him go."

"We've got about seventy-five seconds to get out of here," he said to her. "They're right behind me. But I'm not leaving without it."

"I've got it," Jules said. "So let go of March, and then you'll get it."

March felt his knees go weak.

"Let me see it."

"Let him go."

Oscar twisted the material tighter.

They heard the sound of running footsteps.

Jules tossed the necklace at Oscar. She tossed it high and hard. He had to drop March's shirt collar to scramble after it. It hit the hard stone floor and came apart. The huge amber stone slid and the moonstones rolled as if trying to make a break for *North American Mammals*.

Oscar threw himself at the amber gem, snatching it up and then taking off into the dark gallery. The security guards collided, some diving for the gem too late, others going after Oscar. For the moment they didn't pay attention to the kids in blazers.

Feeling dizzy, March crashed against the dolly. Izzy pushed him onto it. The three — Jules, Darius, and Izzy — gave a great heave. The dolly went flying. Glass shattered and crumbled as Teddy and the dolly smashed through the door.

34

THE MOONSTONES HAVE NO MERCY

Alarms rang as Darius shoved the door open the rest of the way, pushed Izzy and Jules through, and half dragged, half pushed March off the dolly into the cool night air. One guard leaped through over the glass and charged after them.

March staggered, trying to gulp air while he ran, stumbling up a driveway and then alongside the grand staircase in the front of the museum. Cop cars were parked at crazy angles near the front entrance. A TV van screeched to a halt, and a reporter and cameraman vaulted out.

Now that they were among a crowd, they slowed their run to a brisk walk. Security guards ran out, scanning the crowd.

March saw one cop speaking into a walkie-talkie. The cop looked over at them. He did a slow double take as he took in the fact that Jules was wearing a leotard and tights with a short, filmy skirt.

"Uh-oh," March breathed.

"What do we do?" Izzy asked through clenched teeth.

"You there! Stop!"

"Run!" Jules said.

Dodging cabs, they raced across Central Park West. The cop's whistle split the air, and two cops took off after them. The four kids leaped over the stone wall and plunged into the darkness of the park.

They crashed down a hillside, stumbling over rocks until they hit a path. They raced along its windings, hearing the cops tear through the shrubbery behind them.

The path wound over an arched bridge. They dashed over it, turned right, and took off across a grassy field. Suddenly they blundered onto a road with traffic.

A black limousine pulled over and a door was flung open. A dark figure leaned over and said, "Get in." It was Carlotta Grimstone.

"Drive, Samuel," she said calmly. "The police have most likely called for backup. Head to Park Avenue and we'll lose ourselves in the other limos."

March and the others crashed against the leather upholstery, trying to catch their breath. On the upside, they had escaped the police. On the downside, they were now trapped in a limousine with a rich, crazy, mean lady who could turn them in.

Carlotta was dressed in a pink satin gown with silver trim. Silver shoes peeked out from underneath the hem, and a blue spangled wrap was tossed around her shoulders. Gems glittered at her neck and wrist and sparkled on her knobby fingers. Her unnaturally raven-black hair was drawn into a severe bun.

She leaned back and looked at them with hooded eyes. "It's time to talk business. Oh, don't look so innocent!" she said impatiently. "I know your father and mother stole my moonstones." She narrowed her eyes. "It was the night of the blue moon. The night of the prophecy — *my* prophecy. *My* fate. They stole it for themselves, and I hope they *suffered* for it."

"Stop the car," March yelled to the driver. He felt tears ball his throat, and he pushed against the feeling, pushed it back against an invisible wall.

"Keep driving, Samuel," Carlotta Grimstone called. She turned to March fiercely. "Remember this: *I* make the rules."

"Why don't you say what you want to say," Jules said, steel in her voice. "And leave the insults and the threats out of it."

"He got rid of the moonstones that very night," Carlotta Grimstone went on. "I know that much. Almost ten years went by. I never found them. Blue moon after blue moon went by . . . You know what a blue moon is, don't you? Two full moons in a month. Rare, and magic. That's where Merlin's moonstones glean their power. . . ."

March's eyes flicked to Jules. The woman was crazy.

"When I had them, they gave me dreams . . . terrible dreams." Carlotta gripped her satin evening purse. "I saw my death, again and again! But at least they pointed me to a fate I could avoid. It turns out death can be cheated if you see it coming. Now I fear that death is coming again. My only chance is the next blue moon."

"Somebody call the psycho ward; an inmate is missing," Darius murmured.

She ignored him. "Your father believed in their power," she said to March and Jules. "That's why he was trying to steal them back. It is a terrible thing to know your fate. He knew that, just as I did." She shuddered. "Terrible . . ."

She seemed to go away for a moment, her eyes unfocused and haunted. "The moonstones have no mercy," she whispered. "Do you know what I mean?"

"No," March said. He could feel individual hairs sticking up on the back of his neck.

She leaned back against the seat again and looked down at March and Jules. "You never have dreams?"

March felt Jules start. He felt a jolt of fear, something a swimmer might feel as a dark shape moved underwater close to him. How did this woman know what haunted him? "Everyone has dreams. So what?"

Her eyes glittered with contempt. "Let's cut to the chase. What I'm betting is that Alfred McQuin knew exactly where all seven moonstones are. You do, too. It takes a thief to catch a thief. I want to hire you."

"We're not thieves," Jules said.

"And that is why you're running from the police."

"What do you mean, lady?" Darius asked. "We were just taking a walk."

She eyed him, and then her glance lighted on Izzy before she gave a dismissive shrug. "I don't care who you two are. So don't speak. This one," she said, pointing at Jules, "comes down from the ceiling like a spider. This one" — she moved her finger to March — "is onstage, opening his mouth like a fish and not singing. And then the lights go out, and that ridiculously vulgar necklace that ridiculously vulgar woman had, with *my* moonstones in it — poof — it disappears. And you are innocent? Please. I'll tell Samuel to pull over and we'll find a police officer to laugh at your story."

"What do you want?" March asked.

"Ah." She nodded at him. "Good. To the point, like a thief with something to bargain. I want my moonstones. All seven of them. I want them in one week. By the night of the blue moon."

"What makes you think we —"

"And I'll pay a million dollars for each one."

March swallowed. "Uh . . ."

"But only if I get all seven."

A streetlight caught her eyes, and he saw the desperate need in them.

"What if we don't know where they are?"

"I think you do," she said. "You are Alfred McQuin's progeny. You must have inherited *some* of his skills, not to mention his penchant for taking what does not belong to him. This is tediously simple. Catch up. The moonstones are mine. I want them. Here is my private number," she said, thrusting a piece of paper into March's hands. "Call me when you decide. Now get out. I want to go home and watch TV. *CSI* is on."

The limousine screeched to a stop. They tumbled out.

"What was that about?" Darius asked, dazed.

"Seven million dollars," Jules and March said together.

35

THE GRIMSTONE DEAL

Jules looked around the dirty, abandoned platform. "Decent place for a pitch, but a lousy hideout."

March pointed to the graffiti on the opposite wall. MATT HENNEBERRY COME HOME DOMINICK PH. "Does that mean anything to you?"

She shook her head. "Nothing."

They sat inside the train car, on the touristy fleece blankets they'd bought in a gift shop. Izzy unpacked the Chinese takeout. Nobody said anything as they passed cartons and chopsticks. The night lay heavy on them. But they were hungry anyway.

"I had it in my hands," Jules said, spearing a dumpling.

"We blew it," March said.

Izzy scooped up some rice. "What happened to you, Jules?"

Jules chewed her dumpling and swallowed. "Oscar was watching the group home," she said. "I saw the car on the next block over. Same dark green Audi that was at the cemetery. Remember, March?"

March nodded. He remembered seeing the car, but he had never noticed it in the neighborhood. That is, if Jules was telling the truth.

"I was looking in the windows when Oscar got back. Pass the sauce, Izzy? The next thing I knew, I was thrown into the backseat." Jules dunked her second dumpling. "He made me a deal. Help him, and he'd help me. We'd do one job; he'd split the proceeds." She popped the food in her mouth.

"So you went."

"There wasn't a choice involved," Jules said. "My hands were tied. Literally."

March looked at her face. He didn't know whether to believe her.

She saw that he didn't trust her, and her face darkened. She concentrated on spearing a spring roll. "He took me to some swanky apartment in the city. He kept most of the rooms locked."

"Could you find it again?"

"Don't think so . . . I was tossed on the floor of the car. He pulled right into a parking garage, and we took some back stairs up to the apartment. He never let me see anything. Shades were always drawn."

"Scary," Izzy whispered. She shivered.

"Yeah. It was."

"You did it, though," March said. "You pulled off the first heist."

"Oscar made me practice with the vacuum pack in the apartment," Jules said. "It was two floors, so he set up a harness and had me suck up stones hanging from the landing. He had the uniforms, the tools; he'd already paid off the night doorman next door so we got away over the roof. . . . I hate to say it, but it was sorta brilliant."

"Yeah, because *Alfie* planned it," March said.

"You mean Oscar stole a plan of Alfie's?"

March held her gaze. "Or you stole it from me."

Everyone stopped chewing. March and Jules stared each other down.

"I didn't." Jules spoke the words quietly. There was no

bluster, no anger in her tone. "And if you're not going to believe me, forget it. I'm gone."

Now everyone stopped breathing.

When you don't know what to do, slow a moment down.

March tried to push past the hurt and the anger at Jules, past the scared feeling and the ache of missing his dad that lay so deep in his heart, all that confusion and mess, and find something real and true. Looking straight at her, straight into her steady gaze, he realized something.

That thing that had been missing? That person who wasn't there?

It wasn't his mom. It was Jules. All along, she'd been that shadow.

It wasn't like he remembered her. But he *knew* her. And he knew she wasn't lying.

"Okay," he said. "I believe you."

Jules gave a short nod, as if they'd made a deal. "Okay."

The oxygen seemed to flood back into the space, and Izzy smiled. Darius picked up his chopsticks. "So did Oscar split the take?"

Jules made a sour face. "No. He said he needed it for expenses. I think he's going to fence a few gems at a time for safety's sake. I knew he was going to sell me out. I figured it was better to steal the Widow's Knot from him and take my chances."

"Then we popped up, and everything went wrong," March said.

"Listen to the two of you," Darius said around a mouthful of kung pao chicken. "Doom, meet gloom. Don't you realize that we almost got away with it?"

"*Almost* isn't good enough," March said. "We have squat."

Darius shook his head. "Not the way I see it. Jules got her hands on the jewels for a second. March figured out a plan to get us in and get us out, and even how to steal the piece. Maybe would have done it if Jules hadn't shown up. *Almost* is pretty good for your first heist when we're a bunch of kids, wouldn't you say?"

Jules grinned. "Watch out. We've got an optimist in our midst."

Darius smiled back, a genuine grin that made March realize for the first time how handsome he was. "Face it — you two have talent. And some old bat-smack-crazy lady offered us a deal for seven million. I figure I'm ahead."

"The moonstones," March said. "Seven chances to be rich." He reached into his pocket. He held up the moonstone. "Six to go."

36

THE THROWAWAY GANG

The stone flipped from his fingers, almost as if it had jumped. It spun in the air. It seemed to capture every bit of the dim light, drawing it in and leaving them in sudden darkness. It hung in the air. March felt an eerie thrill.

Then it tumbled onto the blanket, and it turned into just another gemstone rolling against a paper carton of Chinese food.

"Whoa," Darius said. "That was . . . weird. Wasn't it?"

They all looked at one another, then down at the moonstone.

"Where'd you get it?" Jules asked.

"Alfie. The night he died." March squeezed his eyes shut. He couldn't think of that last moment, the one heartbeat between Alfie dying and being alive, that hinge between having his father and not having him.

All of his crying had taken place when he was alone. He wanted to keep it that way.

"He was fading out," he said, "and he said, 'Follow the falls to day.'"

"What does that mean?" Jules asked.

"No idea. He was pretty out of it by then. Right before that, he told me to wait a month before I found you."

She frowned. "Why?"

He shrugged. "No clue."

The pain of the memory was still searing. Him kneeling next to Alfie, right there, and Alfie looking at him, fading but with that last fierce light in his gaze, and March was saying, *Don't die,* and Alfie was saying, simply, *NO,* getting out that last word in his last breath. The word was *no,* which didn't seem right at all. Alfie had said such a big *YES* to everything.

Jules picked up the moonstone and held it up. "So we have one from the Amsterdam heist."

March nodded. "Oscar has three. One from the vacuum heist you did for him, and you tossed him two tonight."

"Yeah, I guess I should have let him strangle you," Jules said.

"My point is that I'd be surprised if bat-smack Lady Grimstone didn't already offer somebody else the challenge to gather the moonstones," March said. "She wouldn't rely on a bunch of kids, would she? We're just a backup plan."

"And Alfie left you some kind of list of where the moonstones are?" Jules asked.

March nodded. "Plus suggestions for methods. Izzy decoded the target list. There are seven moonstones and six heists. Alfie did one in Amsterdam. You did Michelle Westlake, and we all bungled Dolores Leon."

"All this for moonstones?" Jules asked. She held it up. "Pretty, but it's not a diamond."

"They're not just any moonstones," March said. "They're magic."

Jules sputtered a laugh. "Right."

"It doesn't matter if you think it's stupid," March pointed out. "Grimstone believes it. I'm guessing that ten years ago, Alfie sold them to his fence. They were broken up and made into other jewelry."

Jules drummed her fingers on her leg. "But what do we do now? Where do we go? The police are going to analyze all the security footage from the museum. They're going to ID us eventually — it won't be hard."

"I never thought about that," Izzy said in a small voice. "All those cameras in the museum . . . they saw us."

They were all silent for a minute. They thought of police and judges and jails.

"There's only one thing that can get us clear," March said. "One thing that will make us disappear. Accept the deal."

"Seven million dollars," Izzy said dreamily. "We could go anywhere in the world. Be anything. And have cupcakes for breakfast."

"And a yacht," Darius said.

"Do you think we could do it?" Jules asked. "Really pull off the rest of the heists? What about Oscar?"

"That would be the first heist," March decided. "That's the only way Grimstone would know we're serious. We'd get all three of his at once. Wouldn't you like to do that? Tie *him* up in knots?"

She grinned. "You bet."

"Even if it means you have to be a thief?"

Jules chewed her lip. "I guess I already am."

"We're the throwaway kids," Darius said. "People think we can't do anything. But we could do this. All of us together make something more than all of us apart, right?"

"The Throwaways," Izzy said. "I always wanted to be in a gang."

March felt his skin buzzing, his blood alive and racing. A door opened inside his mind and possibility rushed in. Maybe there really was another way to live. Maybe they could really do this.

"No more adults," March said. "No more group homes.

No more social services. With seven million, we can figure out how to live the way we want. Are we in?"

Silently, they all bumped fists.

"The Throwaway Gang is born," March said. "Let's make a plan."

37

MISDIRECTION

March spread out Alfie's list on the blanket. Scrawled next to the list were the names Izzy had deciphered.

1. PARTICLE ZOO . . . ???
2. ROOM SERVICE . . . HEIN MULDER
3. VACUUM PACKED . . . MICHELLE WESTLAKE
4–5. SURFING MURPH . . . DOLORES LEON
6. WET PAINT . . . BLANCHE POTTAGE
7. PLASTIC REPLICA . . . RENEE ROOTER

"Here's Alfie's list," March explained to Jules. "Methods and targets. Now we know what he was after. Moonstones."

Jules frowned. "What if Oscar didn't steal the list? What if they were working together?"

"Alfie liked to work alone," March said. "But maybe he owed him because Oscar went to prison. When he got out, maybe he found Alfie."

"What happened that night in Amsterdam?" Jules pushed her food away. "Could Oscar have been there, too?"

March thought about the figure on the street.

"Somebody followed me, but I don't know if it was Oscar." Now that he'd seen Oscar in person, he wasn't sure. He'd only caught glimpses in Amsterdam, and he'd been scared. He didn't have a clear memory.

"Tell us what happened. Right from the beginning."

"My bike was stolen, so I was late. Just one minute, but that can mean everything in a heist, you know? I got there and didn't see Alfie. Then I saw someone moving along the roof. I looked down at my phone to check the time. When I looked up again, Alfie was standing close to the edge of the roof, and —"

Jules stopped him by holding up her hand. "Hang on. Did you hear what you just said? You saw *someone* moving on the roof. You mean you didn't identify the person as Alfie?"

"Of course it was Alfie; the next time I looked up, I saw him clearly."

Jules blew out an exasperated breath. "I worked at the Stick and Rag. I know about what you *think* you see and what's actually there."

"Like tonight," Darius said. "We all thought it was you on the cloud swing when it was dark, but it was just a bunch of lights."

"It's called misdirection," Jules said. "So think, March. Did you see Alfie the first time, or someone else?"

March thought about the shadow. It was impossible to say whether it was Alfie. He just assumed it was. And the next time he looked . . . it was only a second or two. Would Alfie have time, if he were that shadow, to get to where March saw him standing?

No.

It was too far.

There had been someone else on the roof that night.

38

THE WHOLE WORLD TIPS

The knowledge lit up his brain, the realization a spear of agony. "It wasn't him!" he cried. "The first shadow wasn't him. I should have known it!"

"And what would you have done?"

"Warned him!"

"Don't you think he already knew someone was up there with him?" Jules asked. "Why do you think he threw you the moonstone? And what about the bike? What if Oscar stole it so that you'd be late? What if you were meant to arrive *after* Alfie was dead?"

March could only sit blinking at her. Jules's gray eyes were holding his gaze. He realized that she was sitting just as he was, cross-legged, her fisted hands on her knees. It was like facing a mirror.

The information seemed to come in bewildering bursts. Like all those TV shows in countries where he couldn't speak the language. He'd sit on the edge of a hotel bed, trying to pick up a word that made sense.

He had thought one thing, and yet things were going on that night that he didn't know.

"You think Oscar pushed Alfie off the roof." The world was tipping; he was sliding; he couldn't find a place to hang on.

Jules's eyes were on his face. "Maybe. Or maybe he really did slip."

"I saw Alfie up there," March said. "He smoothed his eyebrow — it was our signal for me to take off. It was a *warning*!" He pounded his fists on his knees. "Because he knew there was someone else on the roof! He knew he was in danger!"

"That's why he threw the moonstone."

"And the next thing I knew, he was falling."

"So the person who was following you —"

"Could have been his killer."

He felt himself fracture into pieces. He couldn't breathe.

"He didn't fall." Every muscle seemed to throb around that fact. "He was pushed."

"Hold on," Jules said. "Let's just take this slow."

"No." March shook his head. "No. He was. I know it."

Izzy moved closer to Darius. Jules hugged herself. They all sat, waiting for March to calm himself. He was swallowing again and again against the tears in his throat, but they were sliding down his face anyway. All he could think was: *Pushed not fell pushed not fell pushed. Pushed. Killed. Murdered.* Terrible words from TV and books and movies. Not words about his own father.

He dropped his head into his hands and pressed his fingers against his eyes. He wanted to run fast and far.

He had nowhere to go.

"March." Jules touched his knee so lightly, he wondered if he'd imagined it. But when he looked, her hand was there, close to his but not touching it. "This is the one place, the only one in the world, where you're with people who know how you feel. Not *exactly* how. But close."

Izzy moved an inch closer. "Scary things happen."

"The worst wrong things," Jules said.

"Bad, bad stuff in your head," Darius said. "Feels like it'll never leave."

"Terrible dreams that won't go away," Jules said.

"Things you saw that make you want to rip your heart out of your body," Darius said.

"But you walk around every day anyway," Jules said.

Izzy slipped her hand into Darius's pocket. "When I first met Darius, I tried to pick his pocket. He caught my hand quick as anything. He didn't let go." She leaned forward, her gentle, dark eyes on March. "We won't. Let go. Not if you don't want."

A silence fell, a different one, not charged with March's feelings, but something solid and good.

March let the silence sit. Alfie had told him about silence. He had said that most people didn't understand it. But silence can hammer a point, make an enemy, make a friend. Close a deal.

"Okay," he said. "But this changes things. If we want to acquire all the moonstones, we have to go after Oscar. And he's not just a thief — he could be a killer. So that's a reason to back off."

"Or," Darius said, "it's all the more reason to *do* it."

"Alfie used to say that revenge was never a reason to do a job. Ever. *Revenge gets you jail or gets you dead.* So if we do it, we do it without being crazy. If we go up against a killer, we just concentrate on the stones. That's the only revenge I'm looking for. So who's still in?"

"I'm in," Jules said, her voice quiet.

"Izzy?"

Slowly she nodded.

"I'm in," Darius said.

"And if you're going to do it . . ." March started.

Jules raised an eyebrow in a look that reminded him so much of Alfie that he caught his breath.

"Don't do it stupid," they said together.

39

THE CRYSTAL CAVE

The sign outside the door said:

THE CRYSTAL CAVE

FOR ALL YOUR ASTRAL NEEDS

CANDLES, DREAM CATCHERS, JEWELRY, MEDITATION PILLOWS

PROMOTING SPIRITUAL GROWTH AND HARMONY

MASTERCARD AND VISA ACCEPTED

March pushed open the door to the sound of bells. The scent of incense hit his nostrils, and he heard the recorded sound of chanting. The shop was small and cluttered with objects. Signs reading CANDLES, BOOKS, MEDITATION GUIDES, SPIRIT ROCKS all hung from the ceiling and were stirred by a vintage fan propped precariously on a stack of books.

Darius paused by a display of bumper stickers. PYRAMID ENERGY ROCKS! and MYSTIC SPOKEN HERE and I BRAKE FOR YOGIS.

"Oh brother," Jules said.

"That's *om* brother," Darius corrected.

"Did you say your uncle owned this place?"

"I have a lot of uncles," March said. "They're just not related. But, yeah."

A man swept through a beaded curtain. His silver hair was drawn back in a ponytail, and he wore a purple tunic with a pair of loose, wide pants. *"Namaste!"* he said in a strong New York accent. "Just holler if you need anything. We have a special on Arcosanti bells —"

"Uncle Hamish, it's me," March said. "March. Alfie's kid."

He reared back. "Impossible. You're *tall*."

"It happens," March said. "I haven't seen you since Istanbul."

Hamish Tarscher winced and held up a hand. "The emerald that got away." He strode forward and hugged March. "I heard about Alfie," he said in a low tone.

"Yeah. Well."

"He died in the saddle, kiddo. The way he would have wanted. The man was a dedicated professional. Now he's with the light."

March didn't know if Alfie found the light while lying smashed up on some cobblestones, but adults said the weirdest things about death. "This is my sister, Jules."

"Ah. Whoa." Hamish took a step back. "You're . . . together, eh? Are you sure that's . . . *wise*?"

"What do you mean?"

"Nothing. I often mean nothing. I'm so Zen. Hey, you two look alike. Haven't seen you since you were a toddler, Jules. Glad you grew up." Hamish put his hands together and bowed.

"So we've met?" Jules asked.

"Briefly, memorably, at four a.m. a long time ago. You and your brother — you had your own language, two peas in a pod. This way, young yogis. Come into my inner sanctum." He led them through the beaded curtain into the back office of the shop. A woman in a T-shirt and yoga pants was dreamily packing crystal paperweights into a box.

"Jasmine, can you cover the register?"

"You told me to concentrate on the e-commerce orders today," she said. "Change messes up my aura."

"The universe has many paths, and yours leads to the cash register," Hamish said.

"Peace out," she answered with a shrug, and left.

"E-commerce?" March asked. "You're branching out."

"Certain details of my situation changed, and a scrutiny I did not appreciate occurred."

"Cops hassling you?"

"A certain unfortunate propensity to suggest there could be an illegitimate side of my estimable jewelry business."

"Like, you were buying stolen gems."

Hamish shrugged. "Anyway, I decided it was time to pursue my interest in yoga and meditation, and semiretire."

March turned to the others. "Hamish was my father's fence."

Hamish winced. "I prefer *gem advisor* —"

"He would buy the jewelry from my dad, then break down the stones and make new pieces —"

"I'm really into recycling."

"— and sell them to secondhand jewelry shops —"

"Everybody wins," Hamish said with a shrug.

"— or really high-end jewelry brokers. He's one of the biggest fences in New York."

Hamish gestured to the boxes of paperweights, crystals, bells, scarves, brass jewelry, and candles. "This is a legitimate business. The e-commerce alone bought me a nice little condo in Florida. Tell me what you need, young March, and it's yours."

"Did you hear about the grab last night?" March asked. "The Widow's Knot? Anybody contact you about it?"

"Never heard of it."

"It's a rare amber necklace with a moonstone clasp that went missing at the Museum of Natural History. The thief got away. Cops think it might be connected to that Park Avenue heist a few days ago."

Hamish looked jittery. He went quickly to the beaded curtain, peered out, then returned. "I don't pay attention to jobs like that anymore. Too big, too risky. I've got a nice life. They don't have yoga in prison. So, no."

"How about Oscar Ford?" Jules asked. "Seen him lately?"

"Isn't he still in the joint?"

"He was released from prison two months ago," March said.

"Ah. You might want to check his bookie. Oscar never let a big game go by without a wager. Would you guys like some granola cookies? My wife made them. A tad on the sawdust side, but very nutritious."

"Ham, when was the last time you saw my dad?" March asked. "I know he made a trip to New York nine months ago."

"Oh, who can remember?"

March knew evasion when he saw it. He leaned in and smiled. "Try."

Hamish put a hand on his chest. "Oh. My heart. You looked so much like your father right then. Okay, I saw him nine months ago. Right before Thanksgiving. I remember because I was picking up the tofurkey."

"He was here?" March asked.

"Came to see me, bought me a steak. Don't tell my wife; I'm a vegan. But who turns down Keen's Chophouse? I'm not crazy."

Jules stirred impatiently. "What about the Grimstone Heist?" she asked. "What can you tell us about it? You were Alfie's fence back then. He must have come here."

Hamish wiped his forehead. "Yes, he did. That night . . .

not a good memory. I like my mind to be a place of light and peace. That night was very dark."

"Yeah, most of them are," Darius said.

Hamish smiled at Darius for a moment. "Humor arises from discomfort. I forgive you the sarcasm."

"I am relieved," Darius said.

"Tell us about that night," Jules insisted.

"Some things are better not to know," Hamish said.

"Not for us," March said.

40

DEATH BY WATER

"Alfie came to my apartment with you two in tow," Hamish said. "It was four in the morning. He was out of his mind, raving, saying Maggie was gone — drowned, and it was his fault."

"His fault?" Jules's voice was sharp.

"The escape route," Hamish said. "Alfie had grown up around that lake; he knew it like the back of his hand. They were supposed to climb this cliff, then get out through an ice cave to a waterfall. Some kind of secret passage — a rock like a mirror . . . He had planned the getaway the way he always did, scoped it out, timed it . . . but he didn't factor in snowmelt after four days of rain. The waterfall was much bigger than it had ever been. The rocks were wet. . . . Maggie slipped and went backward, right into the falls. Alfie made his way back down. He dived and dived, but never found her. She'd been washed right out into the middle of the lake."

March shot a look at Jules. "Go on," she said, her voice husky.

Hamish got out a large pink handkerchief and blew his nose.

"Wonderful woman," he said. "Could spot a cubic zirconia fake engagement ring at twenty paces. Sad." He cleared his throat. "Anyway. The only thing that Alfie had left was the moonstones. He brought them to me to sell. I was surprised. The man never dealt in semiprecious. Then he showed them to me."

Hamish turned to a locked case. He fished out a key from the necklaces around his neck and fitted it into the lock. "I keep the semiprecious stuff in here," he said. "I've got plenty of moonstones. Some ancient cultures believed that a living presence was captured inside the stone. In India they call them dream stones. If you put one underneath your pillow, you just might dream your destiny."

He spilled out the stones on a black velvet cloth. "And they're just feldspar; isn't it amazing?" He moved the stones around with a finger. "Beautiful. You can see why they're prized. They come in all colors — green, brown, but most are white with that blue sheen. The stone is basically transparent, but within it are these crystal layers — we call them platelets — so light is reflected back out. That's where you get the color. These aren't worth very much. But the seven that Alfie brought . . . I saw how special they were right away."

"Can you describe them?" March had to struggle not to touch the stone in his pocket.

"An especially beautiful *adularescence.* That's what jewelers call that play of light and color inside a stone. With those moonstones, there was a unique deep blue that was inside the stone, but also there was an extraordinary effect when it caught the light — the blue seemed to float over the stone itself. Yes, I could identify the stones, still, after ten years. I can still see them. They took my breath away."

"So what happened?" Jules asked.

"I gave Alfie the cash, and he headed for the airport. I thought he was off his rocker — he kept raving about a prophecy."

March thought back to Carlotta's words about the blue moon — *the night of the prophecy.* Chilly fingers tapped down his spine. "A prophecy? Do you know what it was?"

Hamish didn't meet their eyes. "Hey, who believes in that stuff?" He nervously scooped the stones back into a bag.

"Later I read that the stones came from Merlin's cave. How silly is that?"

March put his fists on the table and leaned forward. "My dad did business with you for over twenty years, Ham. I think he'd want you to help his kids. Tell us about the prophecy. Tell us what he told you."

"Tell us," Jules echoed, leaning forward as well.

"Stop looking like that, the two of you. It's like Alf is in the room! Okay. The stones said that one thief would be captured that night. Oscar got nabbed. The other thief would die. *Death by water, before the moon is set.*"

"Our mother?" Jules asked. Her voice sounded a little breathless. "The moonstones predicted she would drown?"

"I believe we make our own fate, kid. But it's easy to mock a prophecy that doesn't come true. That night Alfie saw two of them happen right before his eyes. Oscar captured, Maggie swept away."

"What about Alfie's prophecy?" Jules pressed.

Hamish bit his lip. "How old are you two?" he asked March and Jules.

"Almost thirteen."

"Thirteen . . . when?"

"In a week," Jules said. "June twenty-nine. Why?"

"Maybe come back then and I'll tell you?"

"Maybe tell us now," March said.

"Look, it's a silly legend." Hamish forced a smile. "You see this shop? Lucky stones, amulets, Turkish beads for the evil eye . . . you think I believe any of it? I believe that it *sells.*"

"Tell us," Jules said.

Hamish looked uncomfortable. "The moonstones told Alfie . . . well . . . that you two would die before your thirteenth birthday. Together."

41

NO SUCH THING AS FATE

"That's not a prophecy," Jules said shakily. "It's a curse."

"And Alfie believed it?" March asked.

"Never would have thought it, but, yeah. I tried to tell him that the moonstones showed him a vision of what *could* be," Hamish said. "That doesn't mean it *will*."

"What were the exact words? Do you remember?" March asked.

"Who could forget? *Before the passage of thirteen years, the two birthed together will die together.* And he saw the two of you, holding hands and falling."

The dream! Of him on a cliff, groping for a hand, and falling through space toward darkness . . .

"Spooky," Ham said, "since he's the one who ended up . . . well. Falling." He turned to Jules. "That's why he had to give you away. To break the curse. If you two didn't meet until after your thirteenth birthday, you'd be safe."

"So why didn't he tell me?" Jules asked. The question was a cry.

"If I can just interject here," Darius said, clearing his throat, "if you believe in some crazy shut-up stuff, you don't *advertise* it. What was he supposed to say to you, 'Sorry, kid, but I think you're gonna *die*'?"

"Falling," Jules said. "I have this recurring dream." Her face was pale, her eyes large and dark gray with fear.

March swallowed against a suddenly dry throat. "Of falling," he said.

“Yes!” She faced him, her eyes wide. “Of a hand . . .”

“I can’t quite catch . . .”

“I’m on a cliff,” Jules said.

“With black water below,” March finished.

Hamish broke the stunned silence. “Coincidence!” he boomed with fake cheer.

“Our birthday is in a week,” he said to Jules, trying to keep his voice even. His stomach twisted with fear. “It’s the night of the blue moon. That’s why Alfie told me to wait a month to find you! Because then we’d be thirteen, and the curse would be broken!”

“We found each other too soon,” Jules said.

“You two are seriously freaking me out,” Darius said.

“Stop it,” Izzy said. She put her hands over her ears.

Hamish stood, his feet doing an anxious dance. “Well, this has been a lovely reunion, but I have a business to run.”

“Do me a favor?” March asked.

Hamish put his hands together and bowed. “You know, as your honorary uncle, I will do you a solid anytime.”

“If Oscar Ford comes around, don’t tell him we were here.”

“Never saw you.”

They pushed through the curtain and went to the exit.

“You’ll be fine!” Hamish called. “Just . . . stay on the ground!”

42

SPOOKED

They sat at an outdoor table at a boutique coffee shop across the street and down from Hamish's shop. Jules and March sat without moving.

Darius cleared his throat. "Ahem. I can see where someone might be slightly freaked by what just occurred," he said. "But that is no reason to believe in a prophecy told by a handful of . . . what did he call it? Feldspar? And Merlin's cave? Come *on*."

"You don't believe it, do you?" Izzy asked them.

"Nah," March said. When you were watching the world go by on a sunny Saturday, everything looked ordinary and fine. Prophecies just seemed stupid.

But he couldn't forget the harrowing dream.

"Of course not," Jules said. She didn't meet March's eyes as she held her warm cup against her cheek for comfort. "Do we trust Hamish?"

March twisted a napkin. "Sure. Just not all the way. Alfie always said I could count on him, but always remember that Ham is a businessman. He's always out for the deal. He lied about the Widow's Knot."

"How do you know?" Izzy asked.

"Because it's on the front page of the *Post*, and he had a copy right by his computer. It's a huge heist — of course he'd know about it. And when he opened that drawer, I saw diamonds and sapphires. . . ."

"The necklace I stole from that reporter," Jules said.

"Ham is Oscar's fence, too."

"He seemed in a hurry to get rid of us," she said. "And it wasn't just because he thought we were the walking dead."

March nodded. "Exactly."

The streets of the East Village were crowded with locals and tourists. In front of the café was a Citi Bike rack, part of a bike-sharing program. The bright blue bikes were lined up in locking stations. A family of four cycled up, guided the bikes into the stations, and the locking mechanism turned green. The family plopped at a table.

"You were right, Doug," the mom said. "It was a great way to get around. But I think we should take a cab back to the hotel. I'm beat."

"You're right. I'll get the drinks to go."

March tried to drown out their conversation and think. They needed a big success. Three moonstones in one heist. They needed to find out where Oscar lived.

"We still have twenty minutes left," the girl whined. "Why can't we bike back?"

"I like cabs," the boy said. "There's one."

Across the street a cab pulled up in front of the Crystal Cave. A handsome, well-dressed man emerged.

"Is that a movie star?" the girl asked, her crankiness gone.

It was Oscar Ford.

A wave of blackout rage, hot and clean, sliced through March. For a moment he couldn't see. He thought of Oscar Ford on that roof, giving a sudden shove to Alfie, pushing him into thin air. Now that man was living his life, grinning at a pretty girl and enjoying the sunshine.

Jules put a hand on his wrist. "Don't do it stupid," she murmured.

Oscar disappeared into Hamish's shop. March let out a long, shaky breath.

The father returned with water bottles. "I'll hail a cab." He reached in his pocket for cash. A piece of paper floated to the floor. March put his foot on it.

It was something he learned from Alfie. *When somebody drops something, don't be in a hurry to give it back. First give it a look. Why not?*

"Oscar won't be long," March said. His mind raced with possibilities. "He's just going to hand over the amber to Ham. I bet he heads right back home. Thieves don't like to keep all that cash in their pockets after a heist. We can follow him."

"How are we going to keep up with him?" Jules asked. "He'll take a cab. Lots of traffic. We could lose him, easy."

March unfurled the paper as the tourist family scrambled into a cab. Written on it were four number codes. He looked at the Citi Bikes.

"Drink up, gang," March said. "I have an idea."

43

CROSSTOWN RACERS

The four bikes the family had used were still locked in the racks. March figured that the paper he held contained the codes to unlock them. It took them three tries before they figured out which code went to which bike. Within minutes they were each astride a bright blue bike.

"Here comes our man," Jules said.

Oscar hurried out of the store. His face was set in a glower. He was dressed in a tight polo shirt, skinny jeans, and sunglasses. His artfully tousled hair was now an even lighter blond than the photo on TV. Several women turned to look at him as he stood in the street, his hand raised to hail a cab.

"He thinks he *is* a movie star." Izzy snorted.

March's hands tightened on the handlebars.

"You okay?" Jules murmured.

Feelings have no place on a job, kid.

"Fine."

A cab swerved over to pick Oscar up. "Jules, you stay back since Oscar knows you best," March said. "Take the lead position first, Izzy."

As the cab zoomed by, Izzy pedaled fast, following the cab as it crossed Second Avenue. They followed, hanging back and keeping Izzy in sight.

The cab turned right on Houston Street.

"He's going west," March said.

The street was crammed with pedestrians, cars, cabs, buses, and bicyclists. March's heartbeat was a crazy gallop in his chest as he weaved through the traffic, afraid of losing the cab. It was hard to stay close and yet keep a shield of other cars between him and Oscar's sightline.

The cab turned left down Broadway. March dropped back, and Darius surged forward. The crowds were thicker, but so was the traffic, and Izzy was able to keep up, riding behind Darius. Jules hung way back, a baseball cap tugged low over her face.

The cab zoomed south and soon the bikes were bumping along the cobblestone streets of Tribeca. March's teeth were as rattled as his nerves. At Varick Street the light turned green, and just as the cab shot forward, a delivery truck stopped as a stretch limousine tried to negotiate the turn. A surge of pedestrians took the opportunity to cross against the light.

"Go, Darius!" March shouted. "I'll catch up!"

Darius tried to navigate through the pedestrians, avoid the limo, skirt the delivery truck, and make it across Varick as the light flashed green and the cars seemed to leap forward as one mass of metal.

A block ahead, the cab made a left turn and disappeared.

March pounded his handlebars in frustration. As soon as the tangle of traffic and people cleared, he shot across the intersection.

They caught up to Darius on a cobblestone street. "Lost him," he said. "Sorry."

"It's okay," March said. "We'll think of a way. We could fan out —"

A car rattled by. Jules closed her eyes. "Cobblestones," she said. "I remember them — the night I was kidnapped. The car bumped like crazy right before we reached the apartment. And when we went by that church before? I recognized the sound of the bells. We're only a few minutes away, I just know it!"

"Do you remember anything else?" March asked, his voice urgent.

"Trucks," Jules said, opening her eyes again. "Things being loaded and unloaded. It was early morning. I remember that sound. Oscar had the window down, and I smelled fresh bread. And then when we drove into the parking garage, I felt something else, something under my feet. Rumbling."

"Subway?" Darius asked.

"Maybe. And one more thing."

"What?" Izzy asked, hopping from one foot to the other.

Jules shaded her eyes and turned to the west, where the glint of blue said river.

"Seagulls," she said.

They started on a block-to-block search. On North Moore Street they found a bakery, and they rode past, hoping Jules would remember another sound, another smell.

"Watch out!" March said, jerking his bicycle back. Up on the next corner, a man stood on a terrace, his hands planted on the railing. His gaze swept the street. It was Oscar Ford.

Scaffolding on a building opposite kept them hidden as they walked their bikes closer.

Jules clutched his arm. "Look. The name on the building."

THE DOMINICK

March's heart pounded. The graffiti on the wall of Track 61! It was as though Alfie had put his hand on his shoulder and leaned in, just the way he used to, and spoke in his ear.

"Matt Henneberry, come home," March said.

44

TO ROB A THIEF

The pizzeria called to them with yeasty, spicy smells. They grabbed a table at the back and ordered a large pie with pepperoni. They kept their voices low, even though the television was blasting the college basketball finals. It was time to plan a heist.

"Let's go over this one more time," March said, taking a bite of pizza. "What did you find out, D?"

"It's a very fancy building," Darius said. Darius had pretended to be a delivery boy who couldn't speak English, and in five minutes of confusion had managed to case the entire lobby.

"If that's Alfie's bolt hole, it's pretty fancy for a hideout," Jules observed.

That was true. It wasn't the little studio in a random neighborhood that March had imagined. "Maybe Alfie needed to park some cash," he said. "An investment."

"And gave the keys to his killer?" Jules asked.

March nodded, his face grim. "Obviously Alfie trusted the wrong guy."

"However Oscar got in, he's in," Darius said. "The name Henneberry is on the penthouse A mailbox."

"PH," Izzy said. "Like the graffiti. It didn't mean Dominick's phone number. It meant penthouse at the Dominick."

Darius nodded. "There are two doormen — one at the entrance and one at a desk near the elevators. There's a service door to the left — probably leads to the parking garage. There's a door closer to the elevator marked STAIRS and a door marked STAFF ONLY. Which, as a brand-new criminal mastermind, I declare to be for staff."

March grinned and reached for another slice. "You're catching on."

"Building next door is being renovated," Jules said, waving a piece of pepperoni. "The scaffolding could help us. Bad news is that there's no subway nearby. I think I heard the rumble of trucks heading for the Holland Tunnel. I'm thinking the getaway will be tough."

"The West Side Highway is just a block away," Izzy said. "The getaway could be easy if we had a car." She shot a quick look at Darius.

"Do you know how to drive?" March asked him.

He looked down at his pizza. "Nope," he said.

March took a gulp of soda. "Look," he said. "I'm not going to lie to you. We've got obstacles. We don't have a grease man — the guy who gets us in. Or a boxman — somebody with the equipment and the know-how to open a safe. So let's hope there's not a safe. We don't have years of experience, and we don't have tech equipment, and we don't have a getaway car. But here's what we do have. We've got the world's best jewel thief living in my head. And we've got Jules, who I am guessing is just as good as Alfie on a roof and also doesn't mind dangling from a blue whale or from a skylight with a vacuum cleaner. We've got Darius and Izzy, who are afraid of nothing."

"I'm afraid of everything," Izzy said in a small voice.

"But you do it anyway," Jules said. "That makes you braver than any of us."

Izzy looked down and smiled.

Jules put down her soda. "I'm still worried about the getaway." She pointed to the sketch March had done on a napkin. "Sure, if we don't trip an alarm, if Oscar doesn't get back early, if there's no nosy neighbor, if the doorman doesn't come up to deliver a package, if . . . It's the *ifs* that get you. What if something goes wrong and we have to get out of there quick?"

"That's the flaw. We need a wheelman," March said. At Jules's puzzled look, he explained, "The guy who drives the getaway car."

Darius slowly lowered his head until his cheek was resting on the table. With his mouth squashed against the formica, he said, "I know a wheelman."

"Would he work with us?" March asked. "What's his name?"

Darius gave a great sigh, ruffling the napkin, which flew off the table and drifted to the ground. He put his foot on it.

"Mom," he said.

45

MY MOM THE WHEELMAN

"Shut UP, shut UP, shut UP!" Mikki Fray shouted as she opened her apartment door and saw Darius. She stamped her foot. "Shut UP! You just show up at my door at seven a.m. and give me a heart attack? Come here and give me a hug!"

Darius dutifully stepped into her arms. "Hey, Mama."

She hugged him hard. "How are you, baby? I missed you so much."

"Me, too."

She pushed him to arm's length. Mikki Fray was only a little taller than Izzy, and built like a motel refrigerator. She wore a T-shirt that read SOMEBODY LOVES YOU IN TAMPA, FLORIDA, and black shorts that showed off muscular legs. Her toenails were bright purple.

She stepped back and smacked Darius on the shoulder.

"Wait one second. What are you doing here? Mr. Pete Swampus, up at the home, said I can't see you unsupervised because I'm a bad influence and have to be approved by my parole officer. So what are you doing here?" She put her hands on her hips. "Don't you be getting in trouble, Darius P. Fray."

"His name is Campos. Not Swampus."

"I know what his name is, but the man is a swampus, am I right?"

"I can't deny that."

"Now introduce me to your friends and tell me what's going on, because I can tell something is going on. I haven't been away that long. Proper introductions, last names, too."

Darius quickly introduced the group. Mikki narrowed her eyes at him.

"You all are definitely up to something. And you're going to tell me all about it. But first, I'm going to fix us some food."

Mikki disappeared into the kitchen, and they heard the sound of plates crashing down from cabinets. "All I got is eggs!" she yelled.

"Eggs are good!" Darius yelled back.

"Then I've got to go out, meet my friend Shonda! I'm taking a Zumba class!" A beat, and then her head stuck out of the kitchen. "I didn't come see you right away because I'm trying to find a new apartment. I'm going straight this time, baby, straight as Robin Hood's *arrow*. And I'm going to get you back."

"It's okay, Mama. How long have you been out?"

"Less than a month. You staying here? Because you can. You can sleep on the couch."

"No, that's okay," Darius said. "We've got a place. Izzy's mother's apartment."

"Okay. We'll eat first, then talk. So don't keep talking to me while I'm trying to cook!"

"Right."

"That's talking!" She grinned at Darius. "I love that boy!" she said to the others, and ducked back into the kitchen.

Darius stared at the empty space. "She's got time to sign up for Zumba, but not to visit me," he said.

"She's got the best of intentions," Izzy said.

"I am well acquainted with my mama's *intentions*."

"Do you think she'll do it?" March asked.

"I don't want her to do it. I want her to get somebody *else* to do it," Darius said. "She's going straight — didn't you hear?"

"You love your mama," Izzy said. "That's nice."

"Listen, she let me down about a thousand times, no lie, and she's been in prison, and she forgets about my existence on a regular basis, but, yeah, you've got to love your mama."

"I don't love mine," Izzy said, after thinking a bit. "I miss her, though."

"You miss the mama you didn't have, not the one you've got."

"We all miss the one we didn't have," Jules said.

Izzy retired to the couch to chew on this, as well as a handful of peanuts she found in a bowl on the coffee table.

In a few minutes a platter of eggs, bacon, and toast hit the round dining table. Mikki put a carton of orange juice on the table and directed Izzy to fetch the glasses.

"You all eat. I already did," she said. "I put cheese and hot sauce in the eggs, which is the absolute best way to make eggs. I'm telling you, I live to feed my boy. You all are coming over here every Sunday night. I'll make you roast chicken. Deal?"

Their mouths were too full to talk, so they nodded. The eggs were amazing. When their plates were cleared, stacked, and in the kitchen, she poured herself a glass of juice and crossed her legs.

"Okay. I'm ready."

"How come you don't think I came just to say hey?" Darius asked.

"'Cause you have the same look on your face you had when you were five and you were planning to cut kindergarten. So. Spill."

"We have a job and we need a wheelman," Darius said. "I thought you could recommend somebody."

Mikki reared back in her seat. "Are you coming into my house and asking me to recommend a *wheelman* to my only *son*?"

"Well, where else am I going to go?" Darius asked.

"You're sitting there telling me that you're going to break the law?"

"Not really."

"Not *really*?"

"We just want to get back what somebody stole from us, that's all."

"That's still stealing."

"Okay," Darius said. "I'm just saying, this guy isn't about to call the police on us."

"And the name of this thief?"

"Oscar Ford."

Mikki's expression darkened. "Sweet Face Ford? Nasty guy."

"Yeah."

Mikki let this sink in. She moved her lips as though she were chewing on something.

"So, can you recommend somebody?"

"Somebody? You know I'm the best."

"So we need second best."

"Let me get this straight," Mikki said. "My own son comes to me, about to pull a job. But he wants a *second-best* wheelman. So what I'm asking myself is, exactly how dumb *is* my son, asking for second best?"

"You just got out, Mama," Darius said. "And you said you're going straight as Robin Hood's arrow."

"So I let my son get a second-best wheelman? Who planned the job? I'm not in unless I know the plan."

Everyone looked at March.

Mikki poured herself more juice. "Start talking, kid."

46

BREAKING IN

SHOPPING LIST:
ROPE
NAVY COVERALLS
TOOLBOX
DOG FOOD
ROOT BEER
CHINESE TAKEOUT

"A silver Lexus? Couldn't you steal something less conspicuous?" Darius asked his mother. They sat outside Oscar's apartment the next evening, watching the front of the building.

Mikki patted the steering wheel. "MD plates, too. Cops won't ticket you if you got MD plates. And I like this location. If the worst happens, we zip right on to the Holland Tunnel. If not, we take a little spin up the West Side Highway, and I'm home in time for *Deadliest Catch*."

March checked the time. He drummed his fingers on his leg. If he was wrong about this . . . well, he'd think of something else. But he didn't have time to be wrong. The clock was ticking down to the blue moon in less than a week.

Darius checked his phone. "Second quarter. Whoa — there's a two-point spread. Nail-biting time!"

He slithered out of the car. Dressed in navy coveralls and a hard hat, he crossed the street and disappeared down the alley.

In another five minutes, Darius returned and jumped in the car again.

"How'd it go?" Jules asked.

"Piece of cake," Darius said. "I knocked out the cable to the whole building."

"NCAA finals," March said. "People are not going to be happy. Especially Oscar."

"You know this for sure, right?" Mikki asked.

"Remember Shannon's program? He's from Indiana. They give you a basketball when you're born. And Ham said he bets on big games."

It took ten minutes for the first resident to leave. An older man in an Indiana T-shirt pushed out the door and stomped off down the street. "Heading for the sports bar on the corner," Darius chortled.

Then a silver-haired woman burst out with her husband. Together they jogged down the block.

They waited, nervously staring at the front door.

At last a frowning Oscar Ford hit the sidewalk and walked east.

March wanted to explode out of the car after him. He wanted to hoist his anger like a sword. Slice him to ribbons with the power of his words. *Murderer! Killer!*

But what would he get out of that?

No. Better to destroy him. Steal his fortune.

"Let's go," March said. He heard his voice shake.

"Remember, if the cops come, I'm taking off," Mikki warned in a cheerful voice. "You babies gotta run for the subway at Canal Street."

"Always count on you to have my back, Mama," Darius said in a sour tone.

March headed across the street with Mikki and Izzy.

With a coiled rope over her shoulder, Jules crossed the street to the adjoining building. With a quick look around, she hoisted herself up on the scaffolding, then climbed like an agile monkey up through the construction site. She disappeared.

They pushed open the door.

March hugged a bag of Chinese takeout to his chest. Mikki had a six-pack of soda.

"We're here for the party in the penthouse," Mikki said.

"Name?" asked the doorman.

"Henneberry," March said.

Mikki leaned against the desk. She'd toned down her look and was wearing a gray cotton sweater and dark jeans. "Louisville's gonna smear 'em. What do you say?"

"Go, Hoosiers."

"You're gonna cry."

"Mr. Henneberry, in penthouse A, has gone out for the evening."

Mikki smacked the desk. "Get out! But he's having a party for the game! I've got his son, Matt here, and my daughter, Clementine."

"My stomach hurts," Izzy said.

"He may be having a party, but there's no cable in the building."

"The Chinese food is leaking!" March said.

Darius strolled through the door in his hard hat. "Cable. Box looks fine outside. Need access to the basement."

March saw one of the surveillance cameras showing Jules jumping onto the terrace.

"The food is leaking on the floor!" March cried.

"Mama!" Izzy whined. "I feel sick!"

"You got any paper towels? Clementine, I told you not to eat all that candy!" Mikki began to fuss with the bag, pulling out Chinese food and napkins. She waggled an egg roll at the doorman invitingly.

"That's okay, ma'am. I already ate din —"

"I'm going to throw up!"

"Can you get the door here?" Darius asked.

"Ow!" Izzy said, picking up an egg roll. "It's so HOT."

"Don't eat that, baby. It's greasy!"

Izzy made a gagging noise.

"Door!" Darius called, impatience ringing in his tone.

The frazzled doorman came around the desk and hurried toward Darius. "Don't let that kid throw up!"

March skirted around the desk and opened the stairwell door.

As it clicked shut behind him, he heard Izzy begin to fake-vomit. He was in.

47

THE GAUNTLET

March took the stairs two at a time. The apartments were all lofts, and double height, and the climb wound around and around. By the time he got to the seventh floor, he was winded.

There were only two apartments on the floor. He headed toward PH A.

The door to PH B flung open. A woman stuck her head out. Her glasses were pushed on top of her head. She carried a newspaper and a cup of coffee and a small gray dog.

"Caught you!" she cried.

March's heart seemed to stop. Everything Alfie had taught him flew out of his head. Had his dad taught him what to say if he got caught by a middle-aged woman holding a crossword puzzle?

"You're not the cable guy," she said suspiciously.

He swallowed. "I'm visiting my dad."

"Ah. My mysterious neighbor," she said.

Wishing for his father's easy charm — how many times had he seen Alfie disarm suspicion with a smile? — March smiled.

Obviously, Jules had inherited the smile. The woman was less than charmed. She frowned. "Never seen you here before."

"I live with my mom. Uptown." He leaned in. "She hates my dad."

"Ha! I hate my ex, too! Your dad probably *is* a jerk, kid. You ever walk dogs? I'll pay you." The woman kissed the dog's nose. "This is Ketzie. And I'm Martha Dermott."

"I'm Matt Henneberry. And, no . . ."

"You know what's going on with the cable?"

"No clue. Listen, I —"

"I heard your dad go out a few minutes ago."

March started to walk backward. "Well, I'll just wait, then. I have a key."

He fished in his pocket, stalling. "Good to meet you, Mrs. Dermott."

"Call me Martha, hon."

"Martha Hon." *Go away.*

"Ha!" She leaned against the door frame and took a sip of coffee. "I like you."

He came out with the key on the I LOVE NY chain. He went toward the knob, fumbling, waiting for her to close the door. He put the key against the lock . . .

. . . and it slid in, and the doorknob turned, and the door opened.

March blinked away his surprise. He had *hoped* the key might work, but somehow hadn't *expected* it to. That's why they'd sent Jules in through the terrace. He waved at Martha Hon and closed the door behind him.

Jules stood waiting in the hall. "The key worked? That means that . . ."

"Alfie really did lead me here. He meant for me to find it." He looked down at the key. "But I never saw any of his hideouts before."

Her mouth wobbled, as though she were trying not to cry. "It's not a hideout. Follow me."

48

HOME

Fully stocked kitchen. Cereal. Pretzels. Macadamia nuts. Licorice.

Jules picked up the jar of nuts. "I love these."

Freezer with ice cream, waffles, Popsicles, ravioli, frozen peas.

"Ravioli is my favorite," March said.

"Mine, too!"

Pantry with Italian fruit sodas.

"I love grapefruit soda," Jules said. "Do you see? It's not Alfie's bolt hole. It's a *home*. For us."

March opened the refrigerator. Not much. A half-full takeout container. Protein drinks. And one bottle of champagne with enameled flowers on the bottle.

"That's Blue's favorite champagne," Jules said. "Was she supposed to live here, too?"

"He wouldn't want to take her from you," March said, shrugging.

"Come and see our rooms."

The bedrooms were down a spiral staircase. One bedroom with books on world history, mysteries, and fantasy. March's room.

One bedroom with drawing pads and pencils and a turntable and a stack of old records from the 1980s.

Jules flipped through the records. "Siouxsie and the Banshees. I can't believe it. And the Smiths! How did he know?"

"He paid attention," March said.

"He promised us a home. And he really did it."

"He really did."

Jules shook her head in disbelief. "It's almost like he's here, isn't it? He chose everything." She put her hand on a wooden hairbrush. "And everything is perfect."

"Where did he come up with all the dough?" March asked. But he already knew the answer. "He'd been pulling a lot of jobs the past two years. He'd disappear for days. Once, he was gone for two weeks. And we were living thin. That's what Alfie called it when we didn't have cash. 'A temporary period of living thin,' he'd say."

Jules sat on the edge of the bed. "To see all this — to imagine that it could have happened . . . we could have lived here, with our dad . . . it hurts. And it makes me mad." She punched a lilac pillow. "This is my favorite color!"

"We never had anything like this. Mostly I had a bunch of rented flats. Hotel rooms."

"But you spent day after day, month after month, year after year with him. How many breakfasts, lunches, and dinners is that?"

"I didn't count." March spoke carefully. Her sudden anger was like a light switch, illuminating the pain in her eyes.

"When you've got a dad, you don't have to. Did he buy you T-shirts and sneakers? Did he take your temperature when you were sick? Did he tell you he was proud of you? Did he *make you laugh*?"

"Yeah," March said. He met Jules's anger with as much gentleness as he had. "He did all of those things."

She crossed her arms and swung one leg hard. "Good for you, then."

"Look around. He wanted to do those things for you, too."

"I get that. But it just makes me feel worse. Why didn't he tell us about each other? Why couldn't we have faced it together?"

"He wanted to protect us. I think that, after our birthdays, he would have found a way to get us here. He probably would have made it a huge surprise. Bought a red convertible and filled it with balloons. Drove us here after a swanky lunch."

Jules gave a reluctant smile. "I haven't let myself remember the good stuff. He was fun. Once when I was five, he came to Paris and took me out for ice cream. For breakfast. The best shop in Paris — he knew the owner, and the shop was open, just for me. Then he played the accordion. Only he was so . . . *awful.* I was laughing so hard. . . ." She started to laugh, and then suddenly she was crying.

March picked up her hand and squeezed it.

"I just wish he'd told me. I just wish I'd known!" She cried harder, sobbing. "It's not fair!"

"It's not fair that he's dead, either," March said. "We should have been here with him. We should have lived this future. Oscar stole it. He's *still* stealing it."

She scrubbed her face with her fists. "We're going to get him."

"We sure are."

They jumped when they heard a short knock at the door.

"Relax, it's Izzy," Jules said. "Oscar wouldn't knock."

They ran up the stairs and looked through the peephole. Izzy was outside, shifting her feet nervously.

"Dog food and root beer make excellent vomit," Izzy said as she hurried inside. "Unbelievably gross. He went for a mop and disinfectant. Did you find the stones?"

March exchanged a guilty glance with Jules. "Not yet. Ready to check out his digital profile?"

"That's what I'm here for."

They crossed to the master bedroom. Alfie's bedroom.

Oscar had made himself at home. Shopping bags were tossed in a corner. Inside the closet was a new wardrobe of designer clothes with shocking price tags. An enormous watch was tossed on a night table. A blue Tiffany box sat there, too. Jules opened the velvet box inside. It had once held earrings, but it was empty.

"Maybe Oscar's got a girlfriend," she said.

March poked his head out of the adjoining bathroom. He held up a pump bottle. "Hair spray! There's a reason his hair is perfect!"

Izzy chortled as she roamed through his history on the computer. "He tried to erase his browsing history, but he forgot to check his backup hard drive. Amateur mistake. The guy's been away for nine years. He needs to catch up." She took out a flash drive. "I'm just going to copy what he's got. I need more time to dig."

Jules checked her phone. "We've got to find the stones. The play-off game is almost over. If you were Oscar, where would you hide them?"

"He doesn't seem like the most imaginative guy," March said.

"Right. Alfie was the mastermind."

They started to carefully go through drawers, looking in socks and pockets.

Nothing.

"His texts show up here," Izzy said. "One is to a phone number, but no name. A text came in this morning: 'Interesting headline. Only four to go.' "

“The headline from the *Post* about the Widow’s Knot,” Jules said. “And ‘four to go’ must mean moonstones.”

“Oscar’s got a silent partner?” March wondered. “Did he reply?”

“He just said, ‘On ice.’ ”

“Seriously?” March and Jules asked together.

They looked at each other.

“He *couldn’t* be that unimaginative,” March said.

“Yeah. He could.”

March thought back to the contents of the freezer. “I hate peas,” he said.

Jules raised an eyebrow. “Me, too.”

49

PEAS AND THANK YOU

They raced to the kitchen. March flung open the freezer door. He grabbed the bag of peas and emptied it out in the sink. Three moonstones tumbled out. They picked up the reflection of the stainless steel sink and gleamed like perfect drops of moonlight. Not quite blue, not quite white, not quite silver, but . . . iridescently beautiful.

Something cool and shivery tiptoed up March's spine.

Jules gave a spurt of nervous laughter. "I don't know why I'm so spooked."

"Maybe because the stones say we're going to die in less than a week?"

"Yeah. Maybe that."

March picked up the moonstones. The tips of his fingers tingled as he slipped them into his pocket. "And now we have four," he said.

"Three to go." With a brisk gesture, Jules scooped the peas back in the bag and put it in the freezer.

March's phone buzzed with a text from Mikki.

OSCAR LEFT BAR. GET OUT NOW.

Panic shot through March. "Izzy!" he yelled. "Gotta move!"

They ran back to Oscar's bedroom.

"Almost done," Izzy said, fingers on the flash drive.

They danced their apprehension as Izzy removed the flash drive and closed the computer.

THE SUCKER IS JOGGING HOME! GET OUT!

"We can't go down the elevator," March said. "He'll see us. Stairs . . ."

"Will just dump us in the lobby," Izzy said.

"Terrace," Jules said. "We can drop into the alley."

"Terrace?" March gulped. "*Terrace?* It's . . . high."

"It's our only shot!"

HE'S AT THE FRONT DOOR
DARIUS IS HERE WHERE ARE YOU

"Just GO!" Jules yelled. "I'll meet you out there!"

March and Izzy ran through the apartment, opened the French doors, and escaped out into the open air. A fresh breeze twirled around them from the river. Everything seemed so tranquil from up here. A few pedestrians walking along, a boat chugging by. It seemed impossible that at any moment a killer would walk in the door.

Jules ran onto the terrace, holding a cable and some fabric. "Oscar kept the rigging." As she spoke, she looped a cable around one of the railing posts, then clicked a carabiner on. "Aerial silk is really strong. It will hold us, but not all three at one time. March, you go first. Your weight will steady it for Iz."

"I'm going to climb down on a *scarf*?" Izzy asked.

March looked down over the railing. He felt his stomach drop. "It's a long way down." He met her gaze, hoping his own didn't reflect his panic. He didn't have to tell her. He saw the same fear mirrored in her eyes. The dream. Falling.

"It's not a cliff," she said. "And we don't have a choice."

His phone buzzed.

ON ELEVATOR
U R OUT OF TIME.

50

A LONG WAY DOWN

Jules's voice rattled with urgency. "Wrap the fabric around one ankle, put one foot over the other like this . . . and just lower yourself down. Go as quickly as you can. I'll be last. Oh, wait! One more thing. Hold out your hands."

March held out his hands, palms up. She took the hair spray from Oscar's bathroom out of her pocket and sprayed his hands. "Old-timer's trick when you don't have rosin or chalk. It'll help with your grip."

He grabbed what felt like extremely flimsy fabric and lowered himself over. The fabric swung and slammed him against the building. Pure, screaming adrenaline rushed through him. The stone of the wall scraped his cheek. *Like the dream.*

"Gently!" Jules snapped. "Hurry!"

Even while wondering how *gently* and *hurry* could coexist, he twisted the material around one ankle, put one foot over the other, and started to slide down. He tried not to look at the brick alley below, tried not to think of his father falling, of the ground rushing up at you before you hit.

He was glad Jules had sprayed his sweaty palms. It helped him keep a grip.

He felt the pull as Izzy swung onto the material, Jules steadying her until she was ready to slide down. Izzy clung so hard that she couldn't move.

Jules gave a quick, startled glance over her shoulder, as if she'd heard something. She looked down at March and mouthed, *Oscar*. He must be in the apartment now.

They had run out of time.

Panic pushed out fear. March slid down the rest of the way, jumped the last few feet, and landed hard. He felt the shock in his shinbones.

He reached up to steady the fabric as Jules swung herself on. Izzy was now halfway down.

Oscar ran out on the terrace. He placed his hands on the railing and looked down. His face was twisted in fury as he let out a strangled curse, a howl of pure rage.

"Come on, Izzy!" March urged. "Hurry!"

Oscar disappeared for a moment.

"Do a drop!" March called out to Jules.

"I can't! Not while Izzy's on the silk!"

Oscar returned. He was carrying a knife.

"Long way down!" he called to Jules. He began to saw away at the material.

March locked eyes with a terrified Izzy. He stood, reaching up, but she was still about eight feet above him. He would have to catch her. He didn't know if he could.

"You've got to let go," he called. He planted his feet wide apart and braced himself.

Suddenly Darius stepped up behind him. "I've got this," he told March. He held up his arms. "Jump."

Izzy jumped. Darius caught her, staggering only a bit.

Desperately March looked up at Jules. As soon as Izzy was safe, she wrapped her legs around the silk, twisted her body, and dived. She dropped four feet. Half of the silk tore, and she dropped another foot. She righted herself, twisting her body again. Oscar now held the silk in both hands.

He began to haul her up. "How high do you want to drop from, Jules?" he taunted. The motion of the silk caused her to swing crazily.

Jules used the motion to kick off from the building. The momentum of the swing sent her toward the wall of the other building.

March gasped as she let go of the silk, flew midair, and grabbed the end of a fire escape with one hand. The other hand snatched at air.

She's going to fall!

March ran underneath the fire escape. She was three stories above him. He couldn't catch her. He would watch, helpless, as she fell.

His brain roared, *Noooooooooooo.*

Izzy gasped, her fist in her mouth. *"Pleasepleaseplease-please . . ."*

He looked up at Jules swinging by one hand. *Hang on. Hang on!*

Jules's face was contorted with effort. Slowly, she swung by one hand. The other one reached out, shaking with the effort. . . .

Like the hand in my dream, shaking . . .

And suddenly he felt the moonstones in his secret pocket, as if they had weight and heat, and it was as though they were *willing* her to fall. . . .

As if they both had walked into the prophecy and tempted it . . .

"NO!" March shouted. "Hang ON!"

. . . And her hand slapped against the railing of the fire escape. She grabbed it. For a moment her cheek pressed against the metal, and she took a breath.

"NOW!" March yelled.

In a series of movements that flowed like swiftly running water, Jules hoisted herself onto the fire escape. She ran down, around and around, grabbed the final ladder, released the mechanism, and the ladder clanged down. She scrambled down and jumped the last few feet.

"You won't get away with this!" Oscar screamed. He turned and ran off the terrace.

"He's coming for us," March said, reaching for Jules's hand.

51

BLUE SUBARU

Oscar charged out of the building, and Mikki hit the gas. She screamed onto the West Side Highway and gunned the engine.

"Nobody back there," she said after a minute.

March removed his face from the car seat where he had buried it. Jules straightened up from where her face was pressed to her knees. Izzy gripped Darius's hand.

"Close." March managed to get out the word. He could still see Oscar's face, twisted in hate.

"Gotta say, when I saw Oscar on the terrace and you all on that rope thing, I got a case of the nerves," Mikki said. "But you pulled it out. Now relax."

Relaxing was out of the question. They opted to breathe.

Mikki drove at exactly nine miles above the speed limit, because "they don't ticket you at nine miles above the speed limit." She constantly checked her mirrors. "He didn't bother to try to follow us," she said. "Everything didn't go right, but you got away, you got your loot, so we're good. Everybody calm down," she said, even though nobody was talking.

Mikki checked the rear view again. She frowned. "I think I saw that blue Subaru back on the block."

As the light turned yellow, she sped up and ran through the red.

"Lost him." Her shoulders relaxed.

"That can't be Oscar," Darius said. "He didn't have time to get to his car."

"Don't go telling me who is tailing and who is not. I'm the wheelman." Mikki turned the wheel, hard, and with a squeal of tires they turned onto Fortieth Street. She gunned the engine, and they zoomed down the street at sixty miles an hour. Izzy closed her eyes and clutched the door handle.

"Mama? Can you slow down?"

"No." She hung a right on Eleventh Avenue. Made a left on Thirtieth Street. A right on Ninth. Some blocks she sped, some blocks she cruised.

Finally she was satisfied. "I'll drop you guys at Fifty-Sixth and Eighth. That way I can make a left on Fifty-Seventh and get back up to the Bronx. I don't want to get caught in Columbus Circle."

"Roast chicken on Sunday, remember?" Darius asked.

Mikki drummed the wheel. "Listen, D, while you were pulling the job, I got a call. There's a job in Florida."

Darius went still. "But you just got out. I only saw you once."

"I know, baby, but I gotta take it."

"What happened to Robin Hood's arrow?"

Mikki's face creased in annoyance. "So Robin Hood's a crook; he's got a crooked arrow. I can't turn this down. It's big money."

"Never heard that before," Darius said.

"Watch your mouth! I'm still your mama!"

Mikki swerved and braked at a bus stop. She twisted in her seat.

"You still my baby?"

Darius had the remote look on his face that March had come to know. "Yeah."

They scrambled out of the car. Mikki peeled off with a honk and a wave.

Izzy slipped her hand into Darius's pocket and leaned against him.

"My dad made better chicken anyway," Darius said. "Used to be a chef in Paris."

"Of course he was," Izzy said.

Just then a car swerved over three lanes of traffic and pulled up in the crosswalk, blocking them. It was a blue Subaru.

52

OR ELSE

A man in a sports shirt, jeans, and running shoes got out of the car. He had the blinding teeth of a media personality.

"It's Detective Mike Shannon!" Darius said. "Whoa, I know you!"

"Of course you do," Mike Shannon said, unwrapping a stick of gum.

"You're going to get a ticket," Izzy said. "Your car is in a crosswalk."

"I don't think so. People like me don't get tickets."

He put the gum in his mouth and chewed the stiffness out of it. Apparently they were required to wait.

"So. You know who I am. And I know who you are," he said to March. "And you," he said to Jules. "And I know you had a conversation with Carlotta Grimstone."

"Is that against the law?" March said.

"Relax, kid," Shannon said. "I'm retired, remember? I just want to talk."

"About what?" Jules asked.

"I was tailing Oscar Ford tonight. He goes to a bar, watches the game, jogs home. I'm about to head home when I see you kids running out of an alley, getting into a Lexus, and taking off up the West Side Highway doing fifty miles per hour."

"Forty-nine," Darius said.

"And I ask myself, why?" Mike Shannon said, chewing.

"And I ask myself, why do you care?" March asked in a pleasant tone.

"I'll tell you why, son of Alfred McQuin," Mike Shannon said. "Ten years ago, a heist takes place — a fortune, right? One thief gets caught, one thief dies, and one thief gets away. Moonstones and a diamond disappear. And one cop, the one who noticed the open window, the boot print that belonged to Oscar Ford — the one who was in on the arrest? He is accused by Ford of stealing the Makepeace Diamond. Never proven, but he stops getting promoted. His career stalls. He goes on to have a better career — even becomes a TV star — but he never forgets Oscar Ford. Because he thinks Ford accused him to conceal the fact that *Ford* had the jewel. He hid it that night, and was planning to fence it when he got out of prison. Can we guess who the cop was?"

"It's gotta be that old blowhard from the TV," Darius said.

Mike Shannon gave him a stone-cold stare.

"What do we have to do with it?" Jules asked. "Sounds like this is between you and Ford. And it all worked out, right? You make lots more money as the host of a TV show than you would have as a cop."

"I'm the *star* of a TV show and a media *personality*, and, no, little lady, it didn't work out. Because my name was never cleared. I know Ford pulled off that penthouse heist, and I know he masterminded the museum job. He's got cash in his pockets. And he's got some kind of plan. You happen to know what it is?"

"No," March said.

"Well, I think you do. I think he's out to steal those seven moonstones back and sell 'em to Carlotta Grimstone. Word on the street is that she wants them bad. And I think you know where they are."

"What are you talking about? We're just kids," Jules said.

"Kids who broke into a high-security building. And I'm guessing, took something valuable. Kids whose daddy knew where those moonstones are."

"You're making a whole lot of noise, but not much sense," Darius said.

"Oh really? I know Carlotta Grimstone picked you up the other night — yes, I was there — and I'm guessing she offered you the same deal she offered Oscar."

"Nah, she was giving us a ride."

"She wants them in time for the blue moon in four days. Because she's crazy and she believes they're magic." Shannon looked at their faces. "I'm not trying to muscle you. I just want to make a deal."

"We don't make deals. We're kids."

Shannon ignored March. "I want him behind bars again," he said. "And since you know where the moonstones are, you know where he'll be. When you know he has seven, you find out where the drop is, and let me know."

"This is all interesting," Jules said. "Barely. But what's in it for us?"

"Try this one: I know your names. The police have run the surveillance tapes from the museum. The pressure's on, and somebody sometime is going to background check those singers. I can make it so your photo IDs disappear, along with fingerprints. I can make you ghost boys and girls. But if you don't help me, I'll just tip off the police that I know exactly who tried to steal the Widow's Knot."

Shannon tucked a piece of paper into March's pocket. Then he spit his gum out onto the pavement. "Think about it."

53

HOMESCHOOL FOR THIEVES

Darius balled up his burrito wrapper and looked around the drafty train car. "I am seriously getting tired of these accommodations."

"Izzy looked up the two next targets — Renee Rooter lives in Connecticut, but Blanche Pottage is a San Francisco socialite," Jules said. "We're going to have to rustle up some fake IDs to get on a plane. And the one place people notice kids is when they're traveling alone."

"Be easier to travel by private jet," March said.

"Don't torture me," Darius said, his hands on his stomach. "I'm full of beans. Things could get nasty."

March grinned. "I texted Carlotta Grimstone a photo of the four moonstones and told her the next target was in San Francisco, but we needed help getting there. We leave for San Francisco in two hours."

"Private *jet*?" Darius hooted. "I haven't been on one of those since my daddy hung out with Bill Gates."

The others rolled their eyes. "Sure, D," Jules said.

"I read Oscar's emails on that flash drive," Izzy said. "He's already booked to fly commercial, day after tomorrow."

"He's not going to give up on the moonstones," March said.

"Or us," Jules said. "He knows we're after all the stones now. And that we ripped him off. "

The thought of Oscar coming after them cast a sudden chill in the air.

"Let's focus on S.F.," March said. "We've got the time

difference in our favor — three hours earlier there. Best if we go tonight, catch what sleep we can, and be ready to go early Sunday morning."

"Just don't ask me to catch a cab," Darius said. "They don't stop for brothers in dreads."

"No worries," March said, waving a hand. "Carlotta is sending her car."

After they'd pushed every button they could push from the backseat in the limo, tormented the driver by asking if Darius could wear his hat, turned the TV off and on, and poured sparkling water into champagne glasses, March got back to business.

"Izzy has researched our two targets — we're lucky because these two have digital trails. We know where they live and about their routines."

"What about the first heist — Particle Zoo?" Jules asked. "We still haven't figured it out."

"I've reached out to someone who might know where the first moonstone is," March said. "FX."

"FX? As in, special effects?" Darius asked.

"He's not your ordinary dude."

"Another uncle?" Jules asked.

"Sort of. He might be able to help. The thing is, he's got this paranoia issue . . . won't answer an email or a text. I had to send a card to a post office box. I'm hoping he'll come through. Meanwhile, let's get these two." March tapped the paper.

"San Francisco is Wet Paint," Jules said. "Let's start there. What does it mean?"

"Details make the job," March said. "Alfie always admired a jewelry store heist in Biarritz. There's a bench in front of the jewelry store the gang wants to rob. The weather's nice; people sit there all the time. So what does the gang do? They paint it, then put a wet paint sign on it. Nobody sits on it, they rob the store . . . no witnesses."

"So . . . we're supposed to paint a bench?"

"I don't know if Alfie meant it literally. The lesson is, when you plan the getaway, you disable the thing that the target or the witnesses might be using. You make it so there's no one around, or you shake someone out of a routine. I think it will make sense when we get to San Francisco. Alfie always used to say, 'The map is not the territory.' It means you can plan something down to the last detail, but until you're actually right in the space, on the street, whatever — you don't know it."

"And what about the Connecticut job . . . what does 'Plastic Replica' mean?"

"Easy. The Tucker Cross. Named after Teddy Tucker, the diver who found it in a wrecked fourteenth-century ship at the bottom of the sea. Gold cross with seven big, fat emeralds on it. The government of Bermuda wants to get their mitts on it, so they buy it. Then one day, about twenty years later, the Queen of England is coming for a visit, and they take a look and find out it's been replaced by a cheap plastic replica. The thief was never found."

"Lesson?"

"Replace the item you're stealing. Chances are no one will notice until you're far, far away. But if Alfie made a replica of anybody's jewelry, I haven't found it. And we don't have time to figure out how to make one. So for the last one, we'll have to reach into Alfie's bag of tricks and come up with his favorite rule."

"What?" Izzy asked.

"Improvise!"

54

LIKE A BAZILLIONAIRE

The plane was a Gulfstream, and it came with a pilot, a copilot, and a self-service kitchen with snacks, sandwiches, and sodas. There was a flat-screen TV and a couch.

"So this is how rich folks travel," Izzy said. "No lines, no hassles . . . just drive up and get on."

"Everything is easier when you're rich," Darius said.

"Money can't buy happiness," Jules said. She tried to look nonchalant, but she settled into the leather upholstery with a sigh and ran her hands down the armrests.

Darius chortled. "Are you crazy? Of course it can!"

Izzy and Darius slept. Jules slumped in her seat, her earbuds in her ears, her eyes closed. But March knew she wasn't sleeping.

He sat down across from her. Outside the window were just thick clouds and thin air. They were suspended, moving so fast they didn't seem to be moving at all.

With her eyes still closed, she said, "You seem so confident we can do this."

"Doubt is something that should be entertained privately."

"Another Alfie quote, right?"

"I think I'm starting to get why he was so afraid." March hesitated. "When I saw you dangling from that fire escape . . . I kept thinking you were going to fall. It was like the moonstones *wanted* you to."

"I've never been so scared." Jules shuddered. "And believe me, I've been up that high before. It's like the prophecy is taking hold of us or something. Like, it's going to *push* us. I felt it, too."

"Maybe he felt it that night. He had all seven. Maybe our mother felt it. Maybe she felt *pushed*." March felt the moonstones then, the weight of them in his secret pocket. "Last night the dream was worse. Scarier. I think it's because I know you now." He swallowed. "Losing you in the dream . . . is harder."

"I know." Jules swallowed. "Alfie believed it. And I think Hamish does. And now I do, too."

March let out a shaky breath. "I think there's a *reason* Alfie was going after the moonstones. It wasn't just the money. I think he was trying to break the curse."

"But how?"

March shook his head. "Maybe Carlotta Grimstone will tell us. Didn't she say she cheated death? If we get them for her, she owes us more than money."

"Good luck with that. She only cares about herself. That's obvious."

They were quiet a moment, their heads back against the soft leather seats.

"Well, if it doesn't work, and we find ourselves in midair —" Jules sat up. "I'll show you some grips. So you can hang on."

"Grips?"

"Circus holds. Give me your hand. Here's a C grip. Wrist to wrist. It's a catch grip. Put your hands over my wrist, index finger like this, yes — so that you have wrist mobility. See?"

March felt her pulse against his fingers. "Got it."

"Here's the triangular locking grip. It's the strongest, but it's not a catch grip; it's a hold grip. Here, put your fingers this way. That's it. Feel how strong that is?"

He looked down at their hands. For the first time, he noticed that the shape of their fingers were the same. A word floated into March's head. *Doo.*

"Doo," he blurted. "That's what I called you."

Jules frowned. Then a grin spread over her face. "Mo. That's what I used to call you. I remember now. . . . I remember *you.*"

"It's not a memory, exactly . . ." March started.

". . . more like a dream that actually happened." Jules looked down at their hands. "We used to hold hands . . ."

". . . all the time."

They raised their gripped hands in the air.

"See?" Jules said. "We won't let each other go. Promise?"

"Promise."

They crashed back into their seats.

"Tell me about Blue," March said.

Jules turned and looked out the window.

"What was it like?" he asked. "Growing up like that? It seems so free."

She twisted to face him. "What was it like, being the son of a thief?"

"Lonely." The word came out before he could stop it. The truth.

Jules sighed. "You know what? If you're a kid and your life isn't normal — if you're different or your family is or your life is — it's just hard. Period."

"Most kids want to run away to the circus."

"It wasn't a *movie,*" Jules said. "It was mud and calluses and being hungry and being afraid and running from police and having things be normal for five seconds before they weren't anymore. It was about feeling dumb because you only go to school for a few months before you're yanked out again. It was looking at other kids and wanting what they had."

"Life with Alfie wasn't so easy. I was alone a lot. I was scared a lot that he wouldn't come back."

"And then he didn't."

"We could make it happen," March said. "We could make everything stick. If we pull this off. We could make a home."

Jules was quiet for a moment. "Do you really think we can pull it off? I mean, never show fear or doubt, I get that, but . . . what do you really think?"

"I really think . . . I don't know," March confessed. "Does that scare you? You're the girl who won't start something she can't win, right?"

"That used to be true." Jules seemed to shrug off her mood like a coat she was tired of wearing. She grinned at him. "Before I realized how much fun it can be to try."

55

GIGI-POO

In San Francisco they took a cab to an exclusive neighborhood called Sea Cliff. Sprawling Spanish-style mansions with red-tile roofs and lush gardens overlooked amazing views of the blue bay, with the orange Golden Gate Bridge in the distance.

"Whoa," Izzy said. "This is one big bucket of heaven."

"This is a very white neighborhood," Darius said nervously. "Maybe I should have dressed as a gardener."

"We're okay," March said. "Let's just walk by the Pottage house and take a look. Izzy, fill us in on the details again."

"Blanche Pottage, socialite in San Francisco. Married, three kids, and her husband is a financial advisor. One of those ladies who is really, really busy and doesn't do anything? The bad news is that there's no record — no photo, no mention, zip — of a piece of jewelry with a moonstone in it. The good news is that she just did an interview for this feature called My Morning Routine on a society blog."

"Anything useful?"

"Her trainer comes at seven a.m. She makes breakfast for her husband and kids, then walks her dog at eight thirty. She always goes alone — she calls it 'me time.' Barf."

"This is it," March said, slowing down as they turned the corner.

They all gulped when they saw the splendid, sprawling mansion. March followed the pitch of the roof, noted the two terraces, one probably outside the master bedroom. No bushes near the house, no good places to hide. In one window the unmistakable sign of a security company with codes and alarms. An invisible fence for the dog. An ornate iron gate across the driveway. Parked inside were a Mercedes convertible and an SUV.

"It's a freaking fortress," Darius said.

"Crackable," March said. *Because everything is,* Alfie used to say.

But he had no idea how to do it.

The curtains were drawn back in a front room. From here March could see a peach silk sofa piled with pillows. On one wall was a huge painting with a gold-leaf frame. A vase was in the window, crammed with dozens of white roses.

He thought of his father, who had a strange sense of honor about his targets. He had moved through the world of the wealthy but never been part of it. He stole from those who had been rich so long, they had forgotten ordinary cares. He stole from those who lived in houses like this, plump with silk cushions and bursting with too much of everything. He stole from those who wrecked the lives of others and dusted off their hands and said, "It's business." March had seen it again and again, in fancy restaurants and hotels, so often, he could smell it: the ease of privilege inherited and unearned.

He was his father's son, and he didn't care that he was stealing something from a woman who would simply call her insurance broker in the morning and buy another gem by Tuesday. He was ready to go.

"Duck!" Izzy said. "There she is!"

"Izzy, chill," Jules said. "She doesn't know who we are."

"Oh. Right."

Blanche Pottage came out the front door, a stocky woman in khaki pants and loafers. In her hand was a leash, and the leash was attached to a very small dog with hair the color of ginger ale. The dog kept yapping and jumping as Blanche tried to get her to quiet down. Her glance slid off them as if they didn't matter: just some kids walking down the street. She made a left at the end of the driveway and then crossed the street.

"Just. Keep. Walking," March said.

They kept on the opposite side of the street as she tugged on the leash. "Behave yourself, Gigi-poo!" she scolded. "Remember, I'm in charge!"

"Did she just say *Gigi-poo*?" Jules asked.

"Is that a dog or a rat with a wig?" Darius asked.

They followed her up a pretty winding road lined with cypress trees that cut through the park. On one side was a golf course. The lawn ended, and the expanse of blue bay and golden hills hit their eyes. A plume of fog lay lightly on the water, but the sun shone.

Cyclists and other dog walkers and runners were out enjoying the morning, and the gang wasn't as worried at being spotted. They moved closer.

"Mommy brought you to your favorite place! Don't you love Mommy?"

The dog yapped and ran in circles.

"Silly you," Blanche said. "Come on, let's find our bench."

"Is she wearing the moonstone?" Jules asked.

"I don't think so," March said.

She walked a little way and chose a bench under a tree with a view of the bay. Blanche took a handkerchief out of her pocket and dusted off the bench. Then she sat down, and the dog yapped at her ankles, then nosed her way to the trunk of the tree.

"Don't take too long, Gigi-poo, I have a busy day!"

March snapped a picture with his camera phone. He got an uneasy feeling as he pinched and zoomed on the photo.

He handed his phone to the others.

"Yeah, I know," Darius said. "It's not a rat; it's a dog."

"Look again. At the collar."

Jules leaned over to peer at the phone. "You've got to be kidding me. The *dog* has the moonstone?"

56

FOOLING THE YAPSTER

"Oh no, bro." Darius backed up a step. "I'm not messing with a *dog*."

Jules grinned. "It's not a Doberman; it's a Maltese. It's the size of your pinky, D."

"You take one look at that dog, you know that dog is *mean*."

"He's afraid of 'em," Izzy said.

"Am not. Just don't like them."

"Uh-huh."

"The question is, how do we get the collar? She doesn't let Gigi out of her sight." March kept his eyes on Blanche and the dog.

"House was protected by an invisible fence," Jules said. "So we can't lure her out of the yard. We were going to break in anyway. What's the difference?"

"The difference is, it's on a *dog*." Frustrated, March leaned against a tree. The air smelled so good here, cool and spicy. He didn't know the names of the trees, and he didn't recognize the flowers. Yet this place reminded him of another city. Every time he reached for the memory, it danced out of reach.

"Why would somebody put an expensive jewel on a dog collar?" Izzy asked.

"Because she's an idiot," Jules said. "What about the Wet Paint? What was Alfie planning?"

"I don't know," March said. "I'm thinking he knew her routine, he knew the bench, and he'd planned to somehow get her to another spot, someplace easier for the getaway, maybe. But I don't know if he knew that Gigi the dog had the moonstone." He felt frustration build. He couldn't figure it out.

"If she walks the dog at the same time every day, we could just grab the dog," Jules said. "How hard could it be? Take off the collar, give her back the pooch."

"Look at all these witnesses," March said. "There's cops on bikes and people everywhere."

"Maybe we could stage a mugging and save her," Izzy said.

Everyone looked at Darius. He stepped back.

"So you all look at the dark guy? No way. I'm not conforming to racial stereotypes. Been there, done that with the pigeon drop."

"We're not thugs. We're jewel thieves. But we've got to figure it out, and do it tomorrow morning. Oscar's plane gets in at eleven a.m." March tilted his head back and looked up at the tree, then out at the landscape. Fog was starting to drift in over the bay. Birds wheeled overhead, diving and circling. He almost got clobbered by bird droppings as they flew by.

Lisbon, March thought. *This place reminds me of Lisbon. When that pack of kids squirted mustard on Alfie's back, and then cleaned him up and tried to lift his wallet. He laughed and tossed them some cash. "Easier just to ask,* pequeninos*!"*

He smiled.

"Uh-oh," Darius said. "Dude has got a plan."

57

SUCH HELPFUL CHILDREN

SHOPPING LIST:
MUSTARD
FOOD COLORING
WET WIPES
PEANUT BUTTER
BOTTLED WATER

That night, as he drifted off in the Grimstone private plane at the airport, hoping for no nightmares, March heard the buzz of a text. He picked up the phone. It was from Mike Shannon.

Good luck.

He turned off the phone. The gang had decided to ignore Mike Shannon for now. If they collected the moonstones, they'd deal with him.

The next morning they all dressed in their navy blazers and white shirts. They combed their hair and dusted off their sneakers.

"Where are we from?"

"Chicago," Darius said.

"Who makes the approach?"

"Izzy."

"Jules? Got the mustard?"

She held up a tube.

“Ew,” Izzy said. “We really made it look gross.”

Jules grinned and tucked it into her pocket.

“And the signal is?”

“ ‘Such a lovely day,’ ” Jules repeated.

“Everybody ready? Okay. Now let’s go get ourselves a moonstone.”

Izzy was the lookout. As soon as she saw Blanche leave the house with Gigi, she streaked across the park and signaled them. Jules jumped from the bench and caught the lowest branch of the tree, then swung herself up and concealed herself in the branches.

Izzy calmed her breath, smoothed her pigtails, and went to sit beside March and Darius.

In just a few minutes they saw Blanche in the distance with the scampering dog. When she saw them sitting on the bench, her mouth tightened.

“Go,” March said out of the side of his mouth to Izzy.

“Oh, what an adorable doggie!” Izzy said, springing up and crouching near Gigi. “Can I pet her?”

Blanche’s smile was strained. “She doesn’t like people.”

“All dogs like me,” Izzy said. She reached out her hand. Gigi licked it, then snuggled closer to Izzy’s ankles.

Blanche tugged at the leash. “Gigi!”

“No, it’s okay. Look, she likes me.” Izzy held out her hand again.

Every time Izzy put her hand in her pocket, she came out with a little smear of peanut butter. Gigi licked her, her tail wagging crazily.

March popped up. “Oh gosh, we’re on your bench, aren’t we? Have a seat.” He slicked back his hair and smiled in what he hoped was a winning way. "I'm Arthur Fairchild, and this is Harry Windsor."

If you want to reassure a rich mark, just name yourself after a British king. Works every time.

"I'm Elizabeth Middleton," Izzy said.

"We're visiting from Chicago. We go to the Dunnington Academy. Wow, this is an amazing city."

"You're lucky to live here, ma'am." Darius slid over, leaving room for Blanche. "That's what we were just saying."

Blanche had hesitated, but the combination of blue blazers, a private school, and the earnest smiles of the group encouraged her to park herself at the end of the bench. She kept a good distance from them, but she sat.

Exactly where they wanted her to. Under the tree.

"Such a lovely day," March said.

Suddenly a plop of bird poop landed on Blanche's creased khaki trousers. "Oh!" she cried.

Another plop, this time on her starched white blouse.

"Oh, OH! Ewwwww!"

One enormous plop on the end of her long, pointed nose.

"NO!"

And one last plop on Gigi's groomed blond fur.

"NO, NO, NO!" screeched Blanche.

The three — March, Darius, and Izzy — all sprang forward.

"Harry, old chum, do you have those wet wipes? Let us help you, ma'am."

"Here." Darius tossed wet wipes and tissues in Blanche's lap.

"I have a water bottle. . . ." March handed it to Blanche, who was picking up the tissues.

Fumbling, she dropped the leash.

"GIGI!"

"Don't worry. I have your dog," Izzy assured her. "And I'll wipe that nasty poop off, too. Bad birds!" she said to the sky.

"Can we escort you somewhere, ma'am?" March asked. "You seem so upset. . . ."

"I just want to get home," Blanche said. "Oh, what a mess!"

"Look," March said. "There's a cab!"

It could have been a stroke of luck, but it wasn't. He'd already paid the cabbie.

"Perfect."

Izzy thrust Gigi into Blanche's arms, along with handfuls of tissues. Darius handed her the water bottle. March helped her into the cab.

"Don't forget your purse!" Izzy said, shoving it on top of the pile of dog, tissues, water, and wet wipes.

They shut the door, the cab roared off, and Jules dropped out of the tree. They all jogged away, hearts pumping, and cut through the park. When they reached the museum, they hailed another cab and tumbled in, breathless.

"To the airport," March said.

Izzy tossed him the collar. He held it up.

The moonstone glowed.

They crashed back against the seats, giggling like two-year-olds in a sandbox full of Jell-O.

"Two more to go," March said.

58

MISSING MOONSTONE

The exhilaration wore off after the toast on the plane — "To Gigi-poo!"

They had two more moonstones to get, and they knew where only one of them was. The blue moon was Friday. Only three days left.

Izzy briefed them on the plane. "Renee Cass Rooter. Super-duper rich. Former model who married a bazillionaire tycoon five years ago. Spent two million on the happily-ever-after wedding. Except they divorced last year."

"Boo hoodle, did they have to take a buzzsaw to the Ferrari?" Darius asked.

"He got the thirty-million-dollar apartment on Park Avenue; she got the mansion in Connecticut."

"Moonstone?" Jules asked.

"A ring. Plenty of photos on the Internet of her wearing it."

March looked at the photo. "Anybody else in the house?"

Izzy leaned forward over the tablet, squinting. "Oh no!"

"What?"

"Apparently Renee decided the memories of her marriage were too painful. So she sold all of the jewelry he'd given her at auction."

March had a sinking feeling. "When?"

Her gaze was bleak. "Yesterday."

"And the buyer of the moonstone ring?"

Izzy shook her head. "Anonymous," she said.

Help me, Alfie. Before the plane touches down, I need a plan, because we have to hit the ground running.

Izzy could not penetrate the auction house's records. "This kind of security, I can't crack," she said. "I'd ask my dad, but last I heard, he was in Peru."

"Too bad mine left the CIA after he bought that island in the South Pacific," Darius said.

"Could we break into the auction house?" Jules asked. "Get Izzy to a terminal somehow?"

March frowned. "There's high security in the big auction houses. Cameras. Security guards. ID check-ins. Plus they have a photo ID lockout list — they have a file on every known jewel thief. It was hard for Alfie to get in without a disguise." March sat up. "Disguise!" he exclaimed, slapping his pockets. He dug out his phone. "Yes! It's FX! He finally answered!"

GOAWAY
RED BRICK 107 BWAY CORNER

"That doesn't sound very welcoming," Jules said.

"With FX, that's the best you're going to get," March answered.

59

FX

They stood outside a reddish-brown building on West 107 Street.

"Nate 'FX' Spender," March said. "He's the best tipster in the business. They call him FX because he never looks the same way twice. As a matter of fact, nobody is quite sure what he looks like. He used to do movie makeup, and now he disguises himself and goes to auction houses all over the US and Europe if there's a big sale of stuff like jewelry or art. He scopes out who's buying. If this was a big jewelry sale in New York, I guarantee he was there. He moves from apartment to apartment, never stays in the same place long."

"So will he help us?"

"If he's in the mood. He's kind of . . . eccentric."

"Like how?" Jules asked.

"Hard to explain," March said, and pushed the button marked U. GOAWAY. "Just be prepared."

He leaned into the intercom until he heard the steady fuzz that meant FX was listening. "It's March. I'm with some friends."

A pause.

"Look up!" March commanded the others.

"Why?"

"Just DO IT!"

They turned their faces to the sky.

"Just . . . don't smile," March said out of the corner of his mouth. He felt perspiration trickle down his sides.

Then they heard the buzzer, and he dived for the door.

"He looks out the window and studies you," he explained. "Then he decides if he's in the mood to let you in. I guess we passed inspection."

They took the elevator up to the fourth floor. March knocked on 4B.

The door opened. The first thing they noticed was the blood. A river of it ran down the man's face. One bloodshot eye hung out of its socket and rested on his cheek. Izzy let out a scream.

"Control yourself, young person," FX said. "The neighbors already think I'm weird."

They walked inside the sunny apartment. The only furniture was a wooden chair and a small table, as well as a flat-screen TV that took up most of a wall.

FX turned to Izzy. "If the eye disturbs you, I can remove it."

"That's okay," Izzy said, looking everywhere but at FX.

"March, I've been waiting for you to contact me. But let me remove my eye before we talk."

The man who returned a few minutes later looked nothing like the specter who had answered the door. He was a slender, tanned man with green eyes and red hair.

If March hadn't also met FX with curly hair, dark eyes, and glasses, and as a balding sixty-year-old, he might not suspect that he was wearing contacts and a wig.

"Your father . . ." FX put his hand out for March to shake. "I'm sorry."

March shook his hand and felt the strength of his grip. To his horror, he felt tears spring up behind his eyes. The suddenness of grief was like running full tilt into a sliding glass door. One minute you were on your feet, the next, you were on the floor.

He dropped FX's hand and quickly introduced the other kids.

FX looked at Jules with interest. "The missing daughter. Alfie spoke of you."

"He did?" Jules tried to keep the eagerness out of her voice.

"Many, many times. Regret, loss, hope . . . that's life. He said you were fearless. And yet . . ."

"And yet?"

"He was afraid for you." He looked at her and March. "Both of you." He paused. "The moonstones . . ."

"That's why we're here," March said. "We're tracking them down."

"Are you sure that's wise?" FX walked to the window and looked down at the street. "These are not ordinary gems."

"Do you believe . . ."

"That they have magical powers? Do you?"

A high-pitched scream came from the kitchen, ripping through the silence of the apartment. March and the gang jumped.

FX didn't flinch. "The kettle. I was making tea."

He disappeared into the kitchen.

"He's weird," Izzy whispered.

"Is he going to come out with a hatchet?" Darius murmured.

"No," FX said, reappearing with a tray. "Just ginger tea. I can see why the money is irresistible. Ten million, isn't it?"

"Seven."

He smiled. "She offered Alfie ten. Desperate people make desperate deals. There is a story. . . ." He began to pour tea. "Fifteen years ago, Carlotta Grimstone was scheduled to leave on a charter flight to Paris. The plane crashed on takeoff. In the confusion she was reported dead. Turns out she did not board at all. A year or so before that, a canyon fire in California destroyed the Grimstone lodge in the spring, a time when Carlotta would traditionally have been there." FX passed around the tea in tiny cups. "She has cheated death at least twice while holding those stones. There are countless ways to live in this world and countless ways to die. If we knew what lay ahead, could we avoid our fate?" He sipped his tea. "Apparently so."

"But if there's a way, why didn't Alfie know about it?" March asked.

"He didn't, not for a long time. But then . . . I found something for him."

He sipped his tea, watching them over the rim. "But before we begin, I need to say that, unlike most thieves, I believe one should take curses seriously. If I were you, I'd wait out the birthday. Stay grounded."

"We already have five moonstones," March said.

"You have?" FX looked worried, not impressed. "The power is said to increase with each stone. And the dread."

March knew that. The burden of them was pulling at him all the time now. He hadn't been able to put a name to it until now. *Dread.*

"And if you steal two more, you'll gain a fortune. But what if you fail? What if you *fall*?"

"You know about the prophecy?" Jules asked.

"I know everything. Enough to say, you kids are in over your heads."

"When you're in over your head, you've got two options — sink or swim," March said.

"Alfie's saying?"

"No. Mine. I'd rather swim. I think my dad would agree."

FX nodded slowly, taking in their defiance, their determination. "Fair enough. Wait here." He looked at March and Jules. "And stay away from open windows."

60

THE SECRETS OF MERLIN

He walked past them to another room. In a moment he returned, holding a large, ancient leather book. He put the book on the table, and March peered at the gold letters stamped on the front. *The Secrets of Merlin.*

"I got this at a rare-book auction. Supposed to be a copy of a copy of a copy, etc. . . . going back to the earliest oral legends. Alfie asked me to keep a lookout for it. Nine months ago he flew here so he could read it for himself."

When he opened the book, the odor of a musty distant age rose from it. "There's an anticurse. Something that's supposed to reverse the prophecy." FX put his finger on the page.

Fortune's wheel reverses,
Thus fortune's child must bide
Till the night of rare moon rising.
The portal opens, eventide.
Time reverses by your hand.
The captured lights returning,
Fate's wheel stops — then begins anew,
Your fate annulled, your future earning.

"Well, *that* explains everything," Darius said as Jules took a picture of the page with her phone.

"Alfie said he had finally found a way to keep you safe. The trick of it is, though, you need all seven moonstones. He was on his way to getting them when Oscar showed up. It didn't matter that Alfie had placed half of what he originally got for the stones in a Swiss account for Oscar. Oscar wanted in on the new Grimstone deal. So Alfie said yes . . . but only if he could be alone with the stones on the night of the blue moon. He still feared that something could happen, even at the very last minute."

"So he could do both," March said. "Reverse the curse and get the money."

"That was the plan. Risky. He would not want you involved in this."

"I think he'd want us to try. Here's the list we have," he said, pushing it toward FX. "We only need to locate number one and now number seven. Number two was the Amsterdam job. He left me that stone."

"What about number seven — Renee Rooter?" Jules asked. "She just sold all her jewelry at auction."

"I know. I was there."

"So you know who bought the ring."

"There were a few minor celebrities sprinkled among the crowd. The successful bidder was some sort of television host of a crime show."

March had a sudden sinking feeling. "Do you know who it was?"

"A burly gentleman with capped teeth named Shannon. Mike Shannon."

61

BAD DREAMS

That night the dream was an exercise in terror. The night was darker, the cliff turned to sheer ice. Now he could see Jules's face, her terrified gray eyes, her hand reaching, straining to grasp his. He felt his foot slip as he grabbed at air. He tumbled down and saw her falling, too.

He woke up shaking and drenched in sweat. He looked around the train car. Darius was snoring, Izzy curled next to him. Jules's blanket was tossed aside.

He left the train car and found her on the platform, sitting cross-legged and watching a train loiter at the platform far down the station. He sat down.

"Bad dream?" she asked. At his nod, she said, "Me, too."

"Alfie would say that you look as wrung out as a washcloth in a miner's camp."

She gave a brief smile. "Tonight it was different. I saw your face. There was ice and rain. . . ."

"Yes! And I had you by the hand. You were dangling . . . and we both fell together."

"We had the exact same dream. People would say it's a coincidence," she said.

"Yeah."

"Power of suggestion."

"Uh-huh."

"But it's not."

"No."

March felt a breeze stir from somewhere down the tunnel. It flickered along the wet ends of his hair. He shivered.

"And Friday is the blue moon. It's two a.m. Today is Thursday. We're almost out of time."

"FX will do some digging for us on the Particle Zoo stone. If anyone can track it down, he can. Tomorrow we'll figure out the Mike Shannon heist. I'm sure he's using it for leverage to get in on the deal."

"Izzy did some research. He lives in a fancy, tech-crazy house about forty minutes north of the city. Security cameras all over."

"Yeah. Not easy. Alfie didn't case this job. He always knew if something was doable. He never took a job that he didn't know he could do."

"So?"

"So . . . I don't know; it made me think I could do it, too. It sort of . . . carried me along. Now I don't know."

"So don't do it like Alfie this time." She cocked her head and smiled at him. "Do it like March."

62

SHANNON'S LAIR

Sometimes when you need inspiration, you've got to reach for cupcakes. March passed around the box for breakfast the next morning.

Something had changed. A sense of gloom had invaded the train car. Time pressed against their backs. Nabbing a collar off a dog had been fun. Breaking into a domestic fortress was a whole other thing. Even the cupcakes didn't help.

Izzy put down hers, half-eaten. "Tomorrow is the blue moon. What if we can't steal the rest of the moonstones and break the curse?"

"I know one thing. We won't have to buy March and Jules a birthday present," Darius joked.

No one laughed.

"Come on. You don't believe in all this stuff, do you?" Darius asked. "Magic moonstones? Merlin? Let's stay real."

March didn't know what "real" was anymore. He felt his fate rushing at him, felt the drag of the stones in his pocket, along with the drumbeat of harsh belief that tomorrow night he could fall to his death.

He cleared his throat. "We need time to plan, time to set it up. We won't be able to hit Shannon until tomorrow. I know it's cutting it close, but it's the day he films his show. He goes in at three p.m. and doesn't get home until eleven. While we plan the heist today, FX will be working on finding the other moonstone."

"I think Shannon's system is hackable," Izzy said. "He

controls everything from his smart phone. If you can get me inside, I can access the security system on his computer and set off some little alarm. Something easy, like a rise in temp that will send off an alert but won't look suspicious. If he checks the system, everything will look okay — I just have to stay out of camera range, but that's not a problem. Then, when he resets, I can copy his code and open the doors."

She picked up her tablet. "Listen to this. Shannon was interviewed by a design magazine. *Shannon is particularly fond of his ability to monitor temperature and humidity, set alarms, turn off lights — even start the dishwasher — from his smart phone. 'I'm now a brand,' Shannon declared with his usual aplomb, leaning back in his Eames recliner, custom upholstered in pony hide. 'TV star/writer/producer/personality. Anything that saves time is no longer a luxury, but a necessity.'*"

"Superhurl," Darius said.

"Okay, so if Izzy can get us in and if we find the moonstone, then what?" Jules asked.

"Then we're stuck up in Snootville with a bunch of local cops looking for us," Darius said.

"I've been thinking about the getaway," March said. "One of Alfie's favorite heists used a sweet trick. A thief goes on Craigslist, and under Help Wanted he posts a job for a road crew. Tells everyone to wear one of those orange safety vests and a blue shirt and show up on a street with a bank that just happens to have an armored-car scheduled delivery. So, about fifty guys show up. The thief is dressed just like them. He steals the cash and melts away into the crowd, looking like every other guy in a blue shirt and an orange vest. Pretty smooth, if you don't count the fact that he ended up getting caught."

Darius frowned. "Nobody's going to mistake us for a road crew. And I look all washed out in orange."

March took a swig of juice. "I was thinking purple Lycra."

SHOPPING LIST:
BICYCLE JERSEYS
HELMETS
CARDBOARD BOX (STOLEN FROM CAPEHART REPAIR BACK ALLEY IN FAIR CORNERS, NEW YORK)
BUBBLE WRAP
SCREWDRIVER
HAIR SPRAY
DUCT TAPE
CLIPBOARD

The village of Fair Corners was a town just forty minutes north of New York City. The superwealthy who lived there liked to use words like *charming* and *quaint* to describe it. Ordinary folks got in their ordinary cars and drove for hours in order to clip the shrubs and clean the tubs in mansions pretending to be farmhouses.

The gang wheeled their rented bikes down the sidewalks toward the road that would take them to Shannon's house. Nerves were stretched tight, and they hadn't said much on the train ride out.

March had looked up "evening events" in the surrounding area. The County Bike Club was holding their annual Start of Summer Evening Meet-up.

"The bike meet-up starts at six, and the route takes the cyclists about a quarter mile from Shannon's house at around seven," March explained. "So if we can get in and out by then, we'll get camouflage when we join the group."

Darius looked down at his bike shorts and bright purple top. "Camouflage? I look like a gigantic grape."

They mounted the bikes and took off. It was a pleasant ride along a curving country road to the address. Shannon's house was concrete and steel, built by a famous architect who had set out to make a "statement about the arrangement of domestic space within intersecting planes." It looked like a bunker on Mars.

"Double-height living area, wine cellar, infinity pool, lap pool, outdoor kitchen, media center, indoor kitchen the size of a soccer field, master bedroom in turret," Izzy said. "Nine thousand square feet."

"Big big," Darius said. "It's one person in a freaking hotel, that's what it is."

"It doesn't matter how big it is," March said. "There's only a few places people keep jewelry."

"So how long do we have before he figures out that you took over his main computer?" Jules asked Izzy.

"Depends on how smart he is. Or how paranoid he is, which is worse. If he checks his phone, his spyware might tell him that the main computer was hacked."

"This one might be tricky," March admitted. His fear had been growing since he'd first heard that Mike Shannon had bought the moonstone ring. He was pitted against a former cop, a guy with a grudge who was expecting Oscar Ford to come after him. Had he bought the moonstone as a taunt? If he let them, March's teeth would chatter with nerves. "Let's go over it . . . one more time."

63

SMART HOUSE

They cycled past slowly. Only one car was in the driveway, a Toyota.

"Housekeeper," Izzy said. "She leaves at six."

"She's expecting the package?"

Jules nodded. "Izzy was brilliant — she set up my number as Capehart Repair. I told her there's a recall on a water-heater sensor and we were delivering new parts."

The property was encircled by a low stone wall. It was easy to lift the bikes over and stash them in a stand of trees near a meadow. Darius pulled on the coveralls over his bike shorts and shirt. Using duct tape, Jules and March quickly taped the box together, then used a screwdriver to punch some discreet holes in it. They unpacked the Bubble Wrap and lined it.

Izzy eyed it fearfully.

Darius took her hands. "Look at that nice little nest March and Jules made. If you get scared or something happens to me, you can always get out. You have a box cutter in your pocket. You hear me, Izzy? *You can always get out.* Nobody's locking you up. Not ever again."

Izzy swallowed. She nodded.

"Okay, then," Darius said. "Time to climb in."

Izzy slipped inside the box and folded herself up, hugging her knees and tucking her head down. When she looked up, her face looked tiny and pale.

"It's only March and Jules's possible death and seven million dollars," Darius said. "And it's all up to you. So chill."

They shut the flaps on her smile.

Darius hefted the box. He walked across the road to the white house and rang the bell. Then someone answered, a middle-aged woman in dark pants and a white shirt. She asked him a few questions.

March and Jules watched anxiously. "Alfie always said you can get away with anything if you're carrying a clipboard and a smile," March muttered. A second later he let out a breath. "She just laughed! We're in."

They waited while the clock ticked. March couldn't shake the feeling that he'd overlooked something. Apprehension skittered along his skin.

He was relieved when Darius hurried out the door a few minutes later.

"Everything's okay," he said as he ran up. "The housekeeper is getting ready to go; she had her keys in her hand when I left. Izzy's okay. I sprayed the outdoor cameras with hair spray, so if Shannon looks back at a tape, he won't be able to positively ID us."

A few minutes later the housekeeper appeared. She got into the car and drove off.

March texted Izzy.

ALL CLEAR GO

A moment later her face appeared on Jules's phone. "Okay," she whispered. "I'm going upstairs. I disabled the camera in the first security quad, but by the time he checks, I'll be in the office."

Darius paced back and forth between the trees. "I don't like this. She was shaking when she got out of that box. And now she's alone."

Just then Izzy popped up again. "I'm in the office. Reset temp in the living room. Booting up computer. Going to put the phone down now."

Long, agonizing minutes passed. Then Izzy's face popped up again. "Okay. Shannon saw the alert, checked out the temp, saw the cameras functioning, so he adjusted the temp and got a green light. I installed the mirroring spyware, so I got the code. I just disabled the rear door and reset the cameras. They're on a loop of empty rooms. Go."

March and Jules ran across the lawn and to the back of the house. Darius would keep watch on the road just in case. Izzy waited for them by the back door. "I'll look in the study," she said.

"We'll take the master bedroom," March said.

They ran across the open-plan living room, with its gargantuan leather sofas, and took the stairs two at a time. The master bedroom was in the turret, a gigantic room with curved walls. Two gray sofas sat by a fireplace. An enormous bed was in the center of the room, piled with layers of pillows. Cascading gray silk draperies rippled at the floor-to-ceiling windows. A gigantic gold-leaf mirror reflected it all. There were three separate closets, all full of meticulously stacked cashmere sweaters, jackets, suits, and transparent towers of shoes.

Jules stopped still. "Speechless!"

On the dresser, a heavy gold watch was tossed onto a tray, along with cuff links. There was a mahogany box on the top of the dresser, and March pawed through it. More cuff links. A hideous pinky ring.

“Keep looking,” he told Jules. “I’m going to try the study next door.”

The sun must have set, because the hallway was dark. March didn’t want to risk a light. He pushed open the study door.

For just a moment he was blinded by the last rays of the setting sun. A blue flash exploded onto the white wall.

A man sat in a leather swivel chair, his back to March, holding up something between thumb and index finger.

It was Mike Shannon, and he was holding a moonstone.

64

THE TROUBLE WITH IMPROV

He swiveled the chair slightly, just enough to see March. He smiled. "Surprised?"

March hovered in the doorway.

"Did you really think I'd fall for the broken water-heater ploy? I was a New York City *cop*, kid." He swiveled again so that his back was to March.

March said nothing. He tried to quiet his thundering heart. He kept his eye on the moonstone, which Shannon was holding to catch the light. The blue sheen that seemed to hover over the stone was hypnotic.

"Though I have to admire whoever had the hacking skills to take over my system. I'll be looking into that."

March finally found his voice. "What do you want?"

Shannon swiveled back and forth in his chair. "What does anybody want, kid? A deal."

March thought of Jules in the next room, searching. Soon she'd be looking for him. He walked forward to stand in front of Shannon. This way he was facing the door.

"What kind of a deal?"

"I was waiting to see who would show up, you or Oscar. I was betting on Oscar. He's got that ruthless streak."

"Maybe I have it, too."

Shannon laughed. "Sure, half-pint."

"This half-pint has got the moonstones. Not Oscar."

"Good for you. And you're going to cut me in on the deal. Fifty-fifty." Shannon looked at the stone. "Because I've got this."

"I thought you wanted your name cleared. Not money."

"I don't care about my good name. Nobody remembers me as a real cop. See all this?" He waved a hand. "Leveraged. I was fired last week. They're running old shows this week. Next week I'm off cable."

"You can find something else."

He laughed. "Kids. You never see dead ends. How am I going to get another deal when this house gets foreclosed? Failure stinks, kid. You never get the smell off."

"Maybe you can sell that tacky pinky ring," March said.

"Such a comedian. What I need is quick money. What you need is a moonstone. Here's the deal. When you set up the meeting with Grimstone, I go along and negotiate. You can't do this by yourselves. Who are you kidding? You're kids."

"We did all the work. Fifty-fifty isn't fair," March said, stalling. Their only leverage with Grimstone was the stones. She would have to tell them how to reverse the curse before they handed them over.

Not to mention that he didn't like being pushed around.

"Fair? Grow up. This is nonnegotiable."

"My dad always said, 'If someone offers you a deal you can't change, you're the sucker at the table,'" March said. "No deal."

"I'm not *asking*," Shannon said with a flare of hard anger. For the first time, March saw the viciousness beneath his weary tough-guy persona.

He pulled out his phone and held it up. "There are surveillance tapes of you in New York, San Francisco, and now here . . . the gang of kids who steal from old ladies, dogs, and ex-cops. What a field day the media will have!"

March shrugged. "So I'll be famous."

"Not to mention how much the local cops love me. If I

hit 911, they're here in under five. And you and your friends are walking out in handcuffs."

"If I walk out of here with the police, so will the moonstones," March said.

"Oh really? Don't think so. Who are they going to believe? A former cop who says you stole gems from him or some street kid? I'm guessing you have the stones on you right now."

March willed himself not to touch his pocket. Shannon smiled and hit a button on the phone.

"Nine," he said.

Jules entered the room. March reached up and smoothed his eyebrow. *Go.* Better if just he got caught. Jules didn't move.

"Your time is running out. And your sister's, too. Yeah, I know she's behind me. You kids are so *dumb*." March heard a beep. "One . . ."

Bright lights and noise suddenly erupted in a carnival cacophony of sound. Downstairs a symphony crashed. The flat-screen TV blazed to life. Gunfire from an action movie startled Shannon. The phone shot out of his hand. The dishwasher on the bar started with a whoosh. The lights strobed on and off rapidly.

The house had come alive.

Jules did a running handstand, then flipped over to come at Shannon, feetfirst, aimed right at his hand. He crashed backward, the moonstone flying in the air.

It seemed to hover, flashing not quite blue, not quite white, not quite silver. . . .

March dived for it. Just as everything went black.

65

TRAPPED

The moonstone dropped into his hands as if it belonged there. He could barely make out the gray outline of the door and the gleam of Jules's pale skin.

Shannon was on the floor, desperately trying to work the phone with his left hand. The other was curled in his lap.

"ONE!" Shannon roared.

Jules was already pressing Izzy on speed dial.

"WE'VE GOT IT. GET OUT!"

As they raced down the hall, they heard the front door slam. Izzy was out. They ran toward the stairs.

A loud, rattling noise suddenly began around them, filling their ears with clatter.

Jules grabbed March. "What is it?"

March whipped around. "The hurricane shutters! He must have programmed it!"

They clutched each other as the metal shutters accordioned down. Locks snapped. The house was completely sealed.

It was now so dark that they could make out no outline, no form. The air pressed against their ears.

In the absolute blackness, March felt disoriented. Was the doorway to the study directly behind him, or had they moved closer to the stairs? Which way was the hall to the turret? He could hear Jules breathing next to him in quick pants. He squeezed her hand, alerting her to the fact that they had to move. Shannon knew his house better than they did.

He was coming for them. The police were, too. Shannon would do as he'd promised — he'd tell the police that March had stolen the moonstones from him. He'd be searched. Their chance to get the money, reverse the curse . . . gone.

He'd be back in a group home. Or juvenile hall.

Or dead.

March tried to think past his pounding pulse. Which way to go?

March heard a small noise off to his right. Shannon. But hadn't the study been to his left?

Suddenly Shannon's voice boomed out from behind them.

"This is a home invasion," he shouted. They could hear the rasp of his angry breathing. "No jury would convict me. I had no idea who I was fighting. It was pitch-dark. And I have a perfect right to bash your skulls in!"

Dead cold fear dropped over March, as annihilating as the darkness. Shannon wasn't lying. He could get away with murder.

He couldn't think. He wanted to run, but he didn't know where he was or where to go. Any movement might tip Shannon off to their location. He was standing behind them. Waiting.

Jules put her lips to his ear. "Move left. Hold on to my shirt."

He grabbed the hem of her jersey. She moved like a cat, a silent, gliding motion. His eyes had adjusted somewhat but he still couldn't see. He had to trust Jules completely. Her hands were slightly in front of her, feeling her way.

"Come out, come out, wherever you are," Shannon crooned.

He was to their right. Jules moved accordingly, speeding up her pace a bit while he was speaking. She was heading to the stairs, March guessed.

It was an excruciatingly slow journey down the hall. Any moment, March was afraid Shannon would come at them from behind. With a chair or one of those bronze bookends he'd spied in the study — something crashing down on their skulls.

He felt the air change, become a bit cooler — the bedroom. They had gone the wrong way. They could be trapped here.

They heard the wail of police sirens.

"They're coming!" Shannon called. "And I'll find you before they get here. There's no place to hide. . . ."

Jules hunched her body over her phone to block out the emitted light.

TURRET BEDROOM

In seconds the reply came.

WINDOW OVERLOOKING BACK MEADOW

"Last chance!" Shannon yelled. He sounded raspy and in pain. Desperate. Now he was moving faster, charging through the upstairs rooms. March heard the slam of a closet door.

March whispered close to her ear. "We're four stories up. Even if Izzy can get the shutter up, how can we get down?"

Jules tugged at the expensive drapes that pooled on the floor. "Looks like they're about twenty feet long," she whispered. "That will get us halfway."

March looked at her, incredulous. "Can they hold our weight?"

A thump came from next door, something hitting a wall. "I think you broke my *wrist*, little girl!" Shannon roared. "Want to see how that feels?"

Come on, Izzy, come on, come on.

Suddenly the shutter on the casement window rattled up. Izzy had come through! In less than a second March had grabbed the handles of the casement windows and pushed them out. Jules was ready. Snatching fistfuls of the curtains, she tossed them out.

March looked down. The curtains came to a stop halfway to the lawn. There was still a good twenty feet left.

"I heard that!" March heard the sound of running. Shannon bumped into something. He was probably trying to program the shutters and run at the same time.

"Quick, before Shannon closes the shutters again. *Go!*"

March grabbed fistfuls of the curtain. He climbed over the side. He swung against the house, and terror gripped him. He looked up at Jules.

How did this happen *again*?

It was like the moonstones were *taunting* them.

"We're supposed to stay on the ground," he said.

"No choice." She swung a leg over the sill. "Go."

The sirens screamed in his ears. He saw Darius and Izzy far below, each of them running with one bike on either side, awkwardly but quickly, bumping over the meadow toward the turret. From up here he could see the police cars turning into the lane.

That gave March the incentive he needed. He scrambled down the curtain and swung above the lawn. He ran out of curtain. It was too far to jump.

Jules climbed out, the material from the other curtain in her hand. She scrambled down, then as March hung on the end of his curtain, she held on with one hand as she wrapped the material of the other curtain around her ankles, tied it, and held out her hands. "C grip!"

March felt the material ripping. He reached out to her.

"I'm going to let go, and you're going to lower yourself down once I'm hanging by my ankles. Then you're going to have to jump the rest of the way. Don't worry; you won't break anything. You'll have about a seven-foot drop. This is all going to happen very fast."

The material ripped again.

"Um, now?" Jules said.

March kept his legs around the curtain but hung on to Jules's wrists. She let herself go, hanging just by her ankles, and he slid down as far as he could until he was hanging free. He felt the amazing strength of her arms as she lowered him down. She was hanging upside down, her ankles secured in the cloth.

The rip sounded like a crack of thunder as he let go and jumped the rest of the way. As the curtain tore, Jules flipped up, grabbed the tattered end like it was a vine, and jumped. She landed on her feet. March had fallen backward, his face to the sky.

She grinned and put out a hand. The sound of sirens screamed in his ears, and his pulse pounded with the near escape. "C'mon. They're playing our song."

66

THIRD RAIL

The police went in the front of the house, so the gang took off on their bikes across the back lawn, bumping down the grassy incline. They hauled their bikes over the stone wall, hopped back on, and streaked down the road.

A four-wheel-drive SUV shot out of a driveway, with Shannon at the wheel. The car was like a tank, and, wheels screeching, it headed directly for them. Behind them a police car turned down the road, speeding toward them.

"He's trying to head us off!" March shouted.

"Woods!" Jules cut her bicycle over to the opposite side of the road.

With the screech of Shannon's brakes and the sound of a police car slamming into a stone wall crashing in their ears, they dropped their bikes and took off on foot through the woods. Keeping parallel to the road, they raced through people's backyards. They leaped over stone fences, dodged behind trees. They saw two cop cars streak by, lights revolving.

As they approached the village, they heard the train whistle.

"We're going to have to make a run for it," March said.

Now they ran flat out, along the side of the road, lungs screaming with pain. They reached the village and swung down the last street as the train pulled into the station. Feet pounding, they made the platform and then jumped on just as the doors were closing.

It took them five stops on the train to stop hyperventilating.

"I thought it was over," Darius said. "So Izzy texts me, says, 'Shannon's in the house.' "

"And Darius texts me back," Izzy said. "He tells me to turn everything on max. Make the house go crazy. Brilliant!"

"That was way too close," March said. "We've probably got a million cops looking for us now."

"Six moonstones gets us nothing," Jules said. "What about FX?"

March glanced at his phone. He must have checked it a hundred times today. Finally there was a message from FX. March inhaled sharply.

"FX says he's tracked down the last moonstone. A heist in Barcelona — before the Amsterdam heist. FX says the method has Alfie all over it. He must have hid it somewhere."

"How about in the apartment?" Izzy asked. "We didn't get a chance to really search it."

"It's the only place. We've got to get back in," March agreed. "We still have a key. That is if Oscar didn't change the locks. We can do it and still be in time to meet Grimstone tonight! Let's just hope we can engineer an easier exit."

"I remembered something about Oscar," Jules said. "When we practiced for the first heist . . . he already knew circus grips. I wonder why."

"Well, that makes sense," Izzy said. "I went through all his emails, and there was this solicitation from some circus camp in Canada. He went there when he was a teenager."

March felt Jules suddenly go still.

He saw the conductor approaching. They'd already given their tickets. Was he just walking through? It seemed to March that he was checking them out but trying to look like a man going through a routine. He went all the way to the end of the car. March twisted to watch him. The conductor spoke into a phone.

"Could be trouble," he said softly to Jules. "This car is kinda crowded. Let's migrate."

They casually walked down the aisle and into the next car.

"The next stop is 125th Street," Darius said. "They could have cops waiting at the station. I know that station — all the platforms dump you at one main staircase. They could trap us, easy."

"We can't give up now," Izzy said. "We only have tonight."

"There's another way," Darius said. "But you have to trust me." He hesitated. "It's about my old man."

"The Somali pirate?" March asked. "Or the nuclear scientist working on the secret government project? We don't have time for this, D!"

"The real one," Darius said. His face was red. "The messed-up dude who took off to buy orange juice and never came back. He was a sandhog."

"Sandhog?"

"He dug tunnels. Worked on the big water tunnel in the Bronx. Worked for the subway. Before he got fired. Before he started leaving all the time. Not my point. He used to take me into the tunnels. Freaked out my mom. But he taught me tunnels, man. You think New York City is sitting on a rock? Nope. It's sitting on top of a honeycomb. So I propose we drop off the back side of the platform right onto the tracks. They won't be looking. If you follow me, you can't get hurt."

"What about that third rail?" Izzy asked.

"If we travel alongside the wall, there's a space to hide when the train goes by, if we move fast. Then we walk to the tunnel before the next train comes. In the tunnel there's an abandoned platform at Ninety-Sixth Street. It has access to the street. You game?"

March looked back through the rectangle of window at the end of the car. Cops were moving down the aisle, weaving with the jerking of the train, their hands on their thick belts.

"We'd better be," he said.

The train crossed the Harlem River, dark below the tracks, strings of headlights along the streets, rectangles of yellow in the buildings where normal people were watching TV or eating dinner. March watched it all pass by, his heart thumping.

The train slowed as it approached the station. The police were halfway down the car. March was afraid to attract attention by moving, but they had to.

"We're not going to make it," he said in a low tone. "Next car."

They passed through the next door. They were now on the last car. Jules's face was tight. She'd said nothing since the conductor passed them.

"You okay?" March murmured.

"Sure."

The door slammed. Two cops stood, their gaze sweeping the car. It stopped on the small clot of people standing at the door. One of them nudged the other. They headed down the aisle.

67

EXPRESS TRAIN OF DEATH

The train slowed and lurched. People stood up to gather their jackets and tote bags and suitcases. The cops tried to push through the bottleneck to get to them. They had seconds.

The platform held people dressed for a night out in the city. It also held two more police officers, standing by the stairs, their eyes moving, sweeping along the windows. Darius pressed himself back against the plastic divider.

"Not good," he said.

Suddenly Izzy let out an ear-piercing scream. "RAT!" she cried.

"EEEWWWWWW!" a woman next to them screamed. "I think I saw it."

People began to press behind them as the train slowed. When the doors opened, they were pushed out like a champagne cork.

"Rat!" the woman shouted to the people waiting, who, understandably, hesitated to enter. Darius pushed through the crowd. The police officers were jogging toward the clump of passengers, their hands holding their batons still against their sides.

Darius threaded through the crowd as the officers on the train muscled their way out. They moved behind him as he used the people as a screen to drop over the edge of the platform on the other side.

Jules slipped down easily and held up her hands for Izzy. Izzy dropped down.

March gave a look backward. The police officers were looking over people's heads, down the platform toward the stairs. One spoke into a walkie-talkie.

He jumped off the platform onto the tracks.

In the tunnel they had a couple of small, powerful flashlights and the lights from their phones. Izzy came behind Darius, hanging on to his shirt. Jules brought up the rear.

"Best-case scenario, we make it to the platform before the train comes," Darius said. "The main thing here is not to get killed."

"Sounds reasonable," March said.

"Just don't step on the third rail."

"Which is that?" Izzy asked.

"There. Don't worry . . . Southbound trains don't enter the tunnel on the right-side track. They take the center or the left. Once, my pops had a party on the Fifty-Ninth Street platform. Got him fired, but it was a party."

"How much longer?" Jules asked.

"I think I just *really* saw a rat," Izzy said.

The ground rumbled under March's feet. "Darius . . ."

"I know. Relax. It will be on the other track."

March twisted around. The light was far in the distance. It was hard to tell. But . . .

"They must have changed the routing since I did this," Darius said, squinting into the darkness. "I think it's on this track."

"What do we do?" Jules asked.

The train's roar thundered, the light suddenly illuminating the gray.

"Run!"

The ground was pitted and uneven. *So easy to trip and fall,* March thought, his foot sliding on gravel. Their flashlights swung crazily. The train's hot breath filled the tunnel, pressing against his back, pushing him into darkness. He could now feel the shuddering vibration of tons of moving steel on the tracks. He stopped to look behind him, hypnotized by the power.

Darius took hold of his shirt collar and yanked him. "You want to be track jam?" he yelled. "Come on!"

The roar was now deafening, but March couldn't plug his ears. He needed his hands to keep his balance as he followed Darius down the dull gleam of the tracks. He stumbled in a rut and almost fell, and the terror that shot through him almost knocked him down again.

Darius pulled him forward toward the platform ahead. He boosted Izzy up in one strong move, then leaped up so that he could extend a hand to Jules. She used it to vault herself up, hitting the platform and rolling.

March could feel the moonstones in his pocket dragging him off balance. How was that possible? They were suddenly so . . . *heavy.* His pack slid, pitching him to one side. He stumbled and fell to his knees.

A horn blasted against his ears. The hot air pressed against his back. He saw Jules's hand, reaching for him. He rose, but he couldn't get to her. The stones in his pocket kept him slow and clumsy. He wasn't going to make it.

It's not a cliff in the dream. It's this.

This is where I'm going to die.

68

HOT BREATH, COLD STEEL

"DARIUS!" Jules screamed. "HELP!"

March could feel the rush of hot air and the weight of all that steel pressing against his shoulder blades. The conductor hit the horn, and the sound was so loud that it shuddered through his bones.

Darius reached down with both hands, grabbed him under the armpits, and yanked. March landed face-first on the platform as the train roared by.

He rolled over on his back, gasping. His heart thudded against his ribs. He felt his whole body shaking.

Jules sat, her head between her knees. "That was . . . scary."

Darius looked shaken. "My fault."

Izzy crawled on her hands and knees to sit near them. Her face was a pale blur. "We made it, okay? We're safe."

Is this worth it? March wondered. He felt the stones, the burden in his pocket.

"It's the stones," he said. "They almost killed me."

Jules lifted her head.

"It's like they're getting heavier. It's like they have a *will.* An *intent.*"

Izzy sucked in her breath.

"That's harsh, Marcellus," Darius said, shifting uncomfortably. "Are you sure?"

Jules lifted her head. "The moon is rising," she said. "The blue moon. That's where they get their power, right?"

March reached into the secret pocket. The stones were stuffed in there now. There wouldn't be room for a seventh. They clicked in his fingers. They gleamed like the moon.

They stared at them, at their glow, at the shifting blue, silver, white luminescence, the floating color that they could not name.

Darius swallowed. "Okay. Now even I'm spooked. They just look so . . . strange."

"And beautiful," Izzy said.

"You can't carry them in your pocket anymore," Jules said. "Put them in your pack." She nodded at him. "We can take turns carrying it."

March felt a kind of freedom as he poured the moonstones into the front pocket. When he zipped it closed, he felt better.

Darius led them up a narrow flight of stairs and through an unmarked door. Another corridor, another turning, and then another door. There was faint light coming from a street above. They looked up through the grating.

Darius leaned his shoulder against it. With a screech, it popped out of the crumbling concrete. He found a plastic bucket and overturned it, then placed it under the opening.

Jules flipped herself up easily. She reached down for Izzy, and Darius boosted her up. A couple of moments went by before Jules stuck her head back down.

"Coast is clear," she said. "Come on up. Toss me your backpack, March."

March tossed the backpack up to her. She held his gaze for a moment.

"I'll be careful with it," she said.

Darius boosted March. He landed in the middle of the

Park Avenue median. Grunting, Darius pulled himself up and out.

Cabs whizzed by. The squares of light in the buildings marched upward toward the just-winking stars.

"Where's Jules?" March asked.

The median was empty of everything except banks of azaleas. A few pedestrians strolled down Park in the evening light. Someone on Eighty-Fifth Street laughed to their companion as they headed east toward Lexington.

"Izzy?"

"She was just here . . ." Izzy said.

March looked around wildly. "Where's my backpack?"

Dread and panic danced a frantic duet. His head swiveled in a desperate 360 view. Down the avenue, the cross street, turning, eyes straining, searching for a slender girl with dark spiky hair and an athletic stride.

Disbelief changed to anguish.

He turned to the others.

"She's gone! And she took the moonstones!"

69

BETRAYED

"She stole the moonstones?" Darius looked as though someone had just batted a line drive directly to his skull. "Jules?"

"She didn't," Izzy said. "No way. She'll come back."

March gazed down the street. He had given up looking. He knew how fast she could run. Bitterness twisted his mouth. "You so sure about that, Izzy?"

"She couldn't!"

"But she did! She's the one who said, 'You can't carry them in your pocket anymore. Put them in your pack.' And stupid me did what she said! Stupid me trusted her! Just when . . ." The awfulness of the betrayal felt like a searing brand on his heart. *Just when we were feeling like family.*

"She's not getting away with this," he vowed.

"She only has six," Darius pointed out. "It's not like she can do much with 'em."

And then the realization flooded through March. He gave a harsh bark of a laugh. "No," he said. "She has the last moonstone. She just didn't tell us she did."

"How do you know?"

March thought of Jules on the train, how she grew more silent as the miles passed. "She thought of something on the train. Think about it — it makes sense. Alfie gave me one. I think he gave her one, too. The one he stole in Barcelona. Somehow she realized it. She knows where it is. Or maybe she knew it all along." He whirled to face Izzy. "Tell me what happened when she came up. Did she say anything?"

Izzy screwed up her face. "She just stood there for a second, staring at the moon."

"The moon?"

"Yeah. There." Izzy pointed to where a fat yellow moon was rising from behind the tall buildings that marched down Park Avenue.

But March didn't see the moon. He saw a poster on a lamppost. He walked closer.

UNDERGROUND URBAN FOLKLORE SPECTACULAR!

JOIN US IF YOU DARE

CHECK UNDERCITYCENTRAL.COM FOR THE PASSWORD

FOLLOW THE STEPS TO THE DREAM VAULT

W SPECIAL GUEST

BLUE

A photo of Blue in her top hat, looking fierce.

IN HER NEW SHOW,

PARTICLE ZOO

"Particle zoo!" March said. "The first heist. Whatever it was, Alfie gave Jules the stone. And maybe it's still with the Stick and Rag Players. Because she wasn't looking at the moon," he added. He stabbed the poster. "She was looking at Blue!"

March strode down the street, his steps quickened by fury. Darius kept pace with him while Izzy tried to walk and use her phone at the same time.

"Slow down, man," Darius said. "I'm thinking that Jules must have had a reason to take off without telling us."

"She had *seven million* reasons!" March spit out. "They must have been working on the Particle Zoo show when Alfie saw them back in Amsterdam. Why didn't Jules tell us she knew what it meant?"

Izzy tugged on his arm. "March, on the train — remember when she got quiet? It was right after I talked about Oscar. And the circus camp —"

"I don't care!"

She jumped in front of him. "Wait! You need to see this."

She held out her phone. On it was an image.

Two teenage girls, dressed in leotards and tights. A handsome boy between them.

His mother. Oscar. And Blue.

70

TRUST IS FOR CHUMPS

"It's from the circus camp website," Izzy said. "It's been in front of our eyes all this time! Look at the names!"

March focused on the phone. *Maggie and Becky Barnes celebrate a smooth catch with Robbie O. Ford.*

Izzy jogged next to him, trying to keep up. "Don't you see? They all went to circus camp together for three years while they were in high school."

"That means that Blue knows Oscar," March said. "That's why her favorite champagne was in his apartment! So Jules knew Oscar, too. She only pretended to be kidnapped!"

"No! This is proof that Oscar knew Blue, not Jules!"

"You don't know that!"

"I do!" Izzy said defiantly. "Because I know Jules!"

"Iz, you gotta say this looks bad," Darius said. "I know you like Jules — me, too — but . . ."

"For once you're going to listen to me, Darius P. Fray," Izzy said, narrowing her eyes at him. "And you, too, March. Maybe she remembered something. Maybe she took off." She stamped her foot. "But she is *not* double-crossing us!"

March shook his head. He couldn't think. He didn't know what to believe.

"It's what *trust* is," Izzy said. "Isn't that what we're about?"

Bitterness was acid in his mouth. "Trust is for chumps," March said. "All I know is, I'm getting those moonstones back!"

A man in a fedora with a large daisy on his lapel stood on the corner. It was now close to ten at night, and the usually busy street was quiet except for a group of about fifty young people lingering near a construction shed on the Upper East Side.

The man in the hat had a wire trailing from his ear to his lapel. March heard him mutter into the mic. "No cops around. Ready to roll." He waved an arm at the group. "We're ready. Single file. No photos allowed. Some of you have been on our underground adventures before. You know the drill."

He pushed aside a barrier made of orange plastic netting. Then they packed into a construction shed. Inside was a messy pile of trash on a desk, but it looked abandoned. "They'll be dismantling it tomorrow," he said. "Tonight, we get to play."

He led them to a huge wire cage.

"Down we go," Hat Boy said. "I promise you, it's worth the trip."

They crowded onto the huge elevator. He hit the button, and they lurched down. Down, down, down . . .

"How many stories?" someone asked in a hushed voice.

"We'll be about eighty feet down," Hat Boy said.

One of the young women giggled nervously. "The center of the Earth," she said giddily.

They heard the thump of music as they descended through what they realized was a huge space carved out of rock. It soared like a cathedral around them. Down below, heavy equipment, like huge prehistoric creatures, sat waiting to come to life. Large klieg lights illuminated the space, throwing dramatic shadows.

"Welcome to the Second Avenue Subway Tunnel Theater," Hat Boy said. "Subway scheduled to open three years from now, give or take. We get to party tonight."

March guessed that about two hundred people were milling below them. The freight elevator came to a jarring stop. They filed off, and Hat Boy pressed the Up button and disappeared into the darkness above.

People gathered around a far platform, where a band played loud, undanceable music that some of them were trying to dance to. Others just walked around, marveling at the space.

"Jules would say this was one amazing pitch," Darius said.

March scanned the crowd for Jules. She had ripped off the stones, but she had ripped something else, too, some fabric that connected him to the world.

His eye followed the tall scaffolding surrounding the stage. He had mistaken it for the tunneling equipment. Now he recognized it. Rigging for the cloud swing.

The lights went out, the music stopped, and spotlights suddenly spun crazily. They came to rest on Blue, high up in the rigging. She wore a corset and a tutu shot through with spangles. Her eyebrows were drawn on, high above her azure eyes. Her blond hair was slicked back with gel. A long froth of tulle studded with crystals wound around her top hat.

"Welcome to Particle Zoo," she said.

71

PARTICLE ZOO

The crowd let out a thundering roar.

Blue threw herself out, spinning on the cloud swing, then flipped over and spun again, finally reversing and letting herself gently hit the ground.

She began to play her ukulele. Her voice was strident and strong. It wasn't off-key, exactly, but somehow you expected it to crack at any moment.

"Oh, quarks, I just don't get you.
I know that you are small.
They measure you in flavors
Like ice cream at the mall.
Truth and beauty are one flavor,
Always were a mismatched pair.
Strange rocks that subatomic vibe
Snaring charm with extra flair."

March caught a blur of movement. Jules was climbing the scaffolding.

"I guess it means you're everywhere
But are you on the moon.
Down here on Earth we struggle,
Stuck in our particle zoo."

Jules drifted down on two ribbons of silk, twining herself

in them and spinning as she drifted closer and closer to Blue, who continued to sing. Blue lost the beat of the song, unable to conceal her surprise.

Then Jules soared over Blue, hanging by her ankles, and plucked the top hat right off her head. She swung back to a platform on the scaffolding and plopped the hat on her head. She bowed.

Darius leaned in. "Look who just showed up."

It was Oscar, threading through the crowd, trying to get closer to the action. Jules climbed down the scaffolding, lifted the hat briefly to the applause, and then took off through the crowd, ripping off the blue crystals and tossing them as she ran, unwinding the tulle from the hat. Audience members let out thrilled screams and dived for a memento.

March caught a flash of pale fire, and suddenly, he understood. "The moonstone!" he cried. "All this time . . . it was on the hat! Come on!"

He took off down the tunnel after Jules. Away from the lights, she was just a shadow moving. Oscar was behind her, and gaining.

March's legs pumped, but he knew he couldn't catch them. Darius was right at his heels, and he could hear Izzy's ragged breathing as she ran. The tunnel was muddy here, and he had to dodge the dozers and borers and the gigantic coils of electric wire.

Jules suddenly stopped short.

Blue had somehow made her way faster — maybe from the many branching tunnels? — and dropped down in front of her, leaping from a bulldozer.

Blue put up a hand to Oscar. "Don't come any closer."

Her voice echoed in the tunnel. March crept forward.

"You're not going to harm this girl," Blue called. "Everybody just . . . calm down."

"That little girl stole my rocks, lady," Oscar said.

"Rocks? Jules?"

"Why are you acting like you don't know each other?" March called out. "Back when you were Becky Barnes?"

"What?" Jules asked. She looked confused. "You know him, Blue?"

"Once, a long time ago." Blue lifted her chin. "So what? My sister consorted with criminals. I met a few. But what are you doing, Jules? Why did you . . ." She took a breath. "The hat. You're after the moonstones, aren't you?"

"Alfie gave me a moonstone," Jules said. "I didn't figure it out until today."

"Wait. Now you have all seven?" Blue asked.

"I have all seven."

March's gaze went from Blue to Jules and back again. It was clear that Jules hadn't known that Blue knew Oscar. But who was fooling who?

Blue put her arm around Jules. "But, darling, they don't belong to you," she said. "You see, you have to give them up. Do you want to be a thief like your mother? Die that kind of death? Is that the life you want?"

Jules hesitated.

Blue held out her hand. "Jules. I . . . I know I was careless and distant sometimes. But I do love you. I took you in and gave you the only life I knew. And I'll protect you. Give me the stones. We'll solve this together."

"But . . . there's a prophecy."

"I know all about the prophecy. Alfie told me about it ten years ago. It was a tale told by a con man who wanted to get rid of a child —"

"No!" March shouted.

"You don't want to be like him. Or your mother. Choose me. Choose family."

A sudden thought pierced March. If Blue truly cared about Jules . . . shouldn't she care about March, too? She was his aunt. She'd barely given him a glance at the airport, or here. . . .

March saw naked emotion on Jules's face. He recognized it because it lived in him. Yearning. The need to believe.

Believe against the odds.

Believe you are loved.

"Enough of this, Blue," Oscar growled, and took a step forward. "Give me the stones, kid."

"Stay *back*, Oscar!" Blue held up a hand, and in that gesture, in the commanding look she gave Oscar, in the way he obeyed, March suddenly saw it all. He saw that Blue was not just the ringleader of the Stick and Rag, but Oscar, too.

They were in this together.

Which meant . . .

. . . she was a liar and a fake . . .

. . . and a thief.

"Jules, don't!" March shouted.

But Jules dug into her pocket. She spilled out the moonstones into Blue's palm.

"You made the right choice," Blue said. She withdrew a small silk pouch from her pocket and dumped in the stones.

No, no, no, no . . .

And she tossed the pouch to Oscar.

"Sorry, darling," she said to Jules.

Jules went very still. "You'd sell me out for seven million dollars?" she asked.

"Ten million," Blue said. "We struck a better deal."

72

KEEP ON WALKING

They made it to the surface, Jules crying hard all the way. Izzy leaned her head on Jules's shoulder. Darius hung close, his big hands dangling.

"It's okay, Jules," he said. "You didn't know she'd double-cross you."

"I thought she meant it," Jules said. "I thought . . . I thought maybe she finally wanted me. All my life, I felt like some kind of burden. The Stick and Rag people are the ones who took care of me. Blue was the star. So I thought . . . she really wanted *me*."

"You traded seven million dollars for family?" Darius asked.

Jules wiped her wet cheeks with her fists. "Wouldn't you?"

"Actually? No," Darius said.

The elevator let them out in the abandoned construction hut. They walked out to the cool night air of Second Avenue.

"I remembered the last moonstone," Jules said. "I can't believe it took me so long. Alfie gave me so many jewels — fake ones. Bags of them. I was in charge of the costumes. I remember him giving me a pretty stone and saying to keep it for myself. What he didn't know was that I was so mad at him, I would do the opposite of what he said. So I sewed it into the ribbon on Blue's hat. When I saw that photo of her on the poster . . . when I saw Particle Zoo . . . I realized what I did."

"You didn't know the name of the show?" March asked.

Jules shook her head. "She never told me. I guess Alfie asked. I never cared what the show was called. I was like a performing monkey. 'Do this, do that, swing up, swing down, don't complain about blisters, be glad for what you've got, Jules!'" She ended in a ringing, cruel tone and then burst into tears again.

"Why did you leave us?" March asked. "Why didn't you tell us what you were doing?"

"I was afraid she knew it was there," Jules said. "I was afraid of Oscar. I thought, if I could just sneak in and get it . . . but I was too late. She was already in costume. I blew it. Blue and Oscar get the money . . . and we lost our chance to reverse the curse. It's all over. I'm sorry. It's all my fault."

"It's okay," Izzy said.

Jules scrubbed her face with her fists. "I was so stupid!"

"Nah," Darius said. "If I told you how many chances I gave my mom . . . well, *stupid* doesn't even cover it."

"She doesn't care about me at all," Jules said. "It *hurts*, you know?"

"Well, you can't choose your family," Darius said.

March stopped short. He looked at his friends. He knew, at that moment, smack in the middle of failure, he found something real. Jules hadn't betrayed him. Izzy and Darius hadn't deserted him.

For the briefest stretch of a moment, the fear dropped away. He forgot he was supposed to die, forgot that a fortune had slipped through their fingers. It was just enough to stand there and shrug at each other at how awful things had turned out. Maybe they were facing disaster. But right now, they were together.

"Of course you can," he said.

Sometimes moments were so true and right, they were embarrassing. They quickly started walking again.

March glanced at the ornate bank clock in front of them. "Two hours to midnight. We're in the middle of Manhattan. No cliffs in sight. Plan A: We stay on the ground and wait it out."

"That's definitely the smart thing to do," Jules agreed.

There was a pause.

"Or, there's Plan B. We could endanger our lives by double-crossing Blue and Oscar, getting the moonstones, reversing the curse, and grabbing the money," March said.

They walked a few more steps.

"Let's try Plan B," Jules said.

73

THE LAST CON

"We need a short con," March said. "The simpler the better. Bait and switch."

"Bait who and switch what?" Darius asked.

"Bait Grimstone, switch moonstones," March explained.

"We don't have any moonstones," Jules pointed out.

"I know someone who does."

March punched out Hamish's number. When Hamish answered the phone, he sounded groggy.

"I am asleep," Hamish said.

"Could you wake up for a cool million?" March asked.

Hamish cleared his throat. He sounded more alert when he answered, "I'm certainly open to the idea."

SHOPPING LIST:
SEVEN NOT-MAGIC MOONSTONES
A POUCH

Hamish kept his eyes focused on the road. "I grew up in the city. I'm not the best driver."

"Ham, my man, you are making a million dollars for three hours' work," Darius said. "Relax."

March studied the map on his phone. "We'll have to leave the car on the lake road and go the rest of the way on foot. Hamish is going to meet Grimstone at her house. He'll drive with her to the meeting with Oscar and Blue.

They'll be surprised to see him, but they'll be so focused on the deal they won't care. Grimstone said the meeting spot is on the lake trail. Once we have our hands on the moonstones, we can reverse the curse and make our way back to the Grimstone mansion for the payoff."

"Avoiding the cliff," Jules pointed out. .

"That's key," March said. "Everybody clear? Ham?"

"Let me just get it straight. You called Carlotta and told her *you* had the moonstones. She didn't believe you, but you suggested that Blue and Oscar were about to cheat her. Then after she screamed a while, you suggested that maybe the original fence of the moonstones, who knew them so very well, could authenticate them. That would be me."

"You do have seven unmagic moonstones on you, right?" Darius asked.

"In my right pocket," Ham replied.

"Let's put them in the pouch now," March said. "Jules?"

Jules held out the white silk pouch, and March poured the seven moonstones in.

"Alfie would call this a Plastic Replica," March said. "Darius and Izzy, you clear on the switch?"

"Clear," Darius said.

"If it works, it works," March said. "By two a.m. we'll be millionaires."

"If nothing goes wrong," Jules said.

Nobody had the nerve to add the ending.

And something always goes wrong. . . .

74

RARE MOON RISING

The moon was a silver pathway on the lake.

"'The night of rare moon rising,'" Jules murmured, quoting the curse reversal.

"This is the turnoff, I believe," Hamish said. He steered the car off to the shoulder.

March checked the time. "Blue and Oscar should be at the rendezvous point by now. Remember, they can't know we're there or they'll smell a rat. If something bad goes down, everyone scatter. We'll meet in Fortune Falls in the field by the middle school."

Hamish cleared his throat. "Except for me. Despite the fact that I was an old, old friend of your father, March, I don't do well with incarceration or conflict. So if the worst happens, you can all scatter and regroup. I, however, will stop at Dunkin' Donuts for a coffee and be on the road back to New York."

Hamish took off for the mansion, where he'd meet Carlotta. The gang started down the lake trail. Frogs and crickets gave a steady concert of chirps and deep-throated calls. The woods felt desolate, remote.

March held up a hand, and they stopped. He pointed ahead. He had heard the murmur of voices.

They left the trail and dropped to their knees. They crawled forward through the underbrush.

"If you think this was easy, think again," Oscar said. Oscar and Blue were only a few feet away. They were alone, standing by the side of the road in a little clearing. The Audi was parked on the side.

"I know, you're a hero." Blue's tone was dry. "Look, it's not my fault you went to prison."

"You told me you'd wait."

"I got bored."

"Not funny."

"Not joking."

"Who bought you those sapphires in your ears?"

"You didn't buy *me*, Oscar. I think this might be a time to point out that you almost got skunked by a bunch of kids. *I'm* the reason we're standing here with the moonstones. I'm the reason you stole the moonstone necklace in the first place. I'm the one who figured out how much it meant to that crazy, old bat."

"That was ten years ago. I'm the one who figured out Jules had a stone."

"Yeah, but you couldn't find it. Took apart that sewing machine Alf gave her." Blue gave a short laugh. "And it was on the hat all the time."

"Ten million goes pretty far if you can spend it together. Where do you want to go? Tahiti? Bali? I know an island off the coast of Thailand that will blow you away."

"You still have the mentality of a thief, Oscar."

"That's what I am, babe. You are, too."

"I'm a visionary. You're a grunt. You make the score, you spend the loot, you plan the next job. You get caught, you do time, you get out, you steal again. Nice life, dude. Not for me."

"So, what are you going to do with your take, *visionary*? Don't you owe your niece a piece?"

Jules stiffened.

"Doesn't she owe me? Alfie finds me in London, dumps

the kid, sends me money from time to time, but basically, I had to deal."

Jules flinched. March moved closer to her. Shoulder to shoulder.

"Then after Alfie falls off a roof, they ask me to take both kids but first get a job! The secret nobody tells you is that kids stop you from getting what you want. Maggie wanted kids. I didn't, so why should I have to raise hers? This money is going to launch me. No more Stick and Rag. No more performing in tunnels and warehouses. I'm building my brand and the moon's the limit."

"Vegas, baby?"

"Why not? And by the way, I'm going alone. You should be thanking me for getting you this far."

"Sure. You went to Amsterdam, set up Alfie real nice for us. . . . After he kicked it, you contacted Grimstone, took over the deal . . . figured out the Jules angle. . . ."

"Who knew Alfie's other brat would rustle up his own gang?"

"The kid lost his father."

"So?"

"Wonder how that happened, by the way. Alfie was always so good on a roof."

"I think I hear a car."

"No, you don't. What happened in Amsterdam, Blue?"

"I've got an idea, Oscar. Let's not talk."

March heard Blue whistle under her breath. One long note, one short. Then she sang a few bars.

"Blue moooon . . ."

March stopped breathing. The person on the roof. The person in the trench coat, whistling.

Blue killed Alfie.

75

THE UNBEARABLE

The smell of the lake was in his nostrils and it smelled like Amsterdam suddenly, the dank of the canal. His pulses pounded. He thought of his father, broken on the cobblestones. The light in his eyes going out. He wanted to run at her, run her down. He couldn't *see*, his anger pulsing all of the light out of his vision. He couldn't see the moon or the stars or the trees.

Had she wanted to kill him, too? That night? A little push into a canal?

Jules knew. She put her hand on his arm and squeezed hard. He knew what the squeeze meant, every word in the pressure of her fingers. *You won't win that way. Wait. We'll get her.*

What did Alfie always say?

Save emotion for life. No feelings on a job.

Revenge gets you jail. Or dead.

He let out a breath, long and slow.

Now they really did hear the sound of a car on the road. It came from behind them, and they flattened themselves on the ground. The black Hummer bumped down the road, weaving slightly.

They crept out of the brush and, keeping to the side of the road, made their way even closer.

Carlotta Grimstone turned off the engine and slid out of the car. She was holding a large manila envelope.

"Where are they?"

"Nice to see you again, too," Blue said.

They could see Blue now as she strode into the glow of the headlights like it was a spotlight. She had removed her stage costume and was dressed in a jacket and jeans.

"Let's see the bonds first," Oscar said. "Ten million's worth, transferable."

Carlotta signaled behind her. "I brought someone to authenticate the stones."

"That wasn't part of the deal."

"Too bad. I'm rich, not stupid."

Hamish Tarscher got out of the car.

"Well, hey, Ham," Oscar said. "Whose side are you on?"

"The one with the checkbook," Hamish said. "Relax, Oscar. I'm just here to make sure everybody gets what they deserve."

"Show him the stones," Carlotta said eagerly.

Blue handed a pouch to Hamish, and he shook out the stones into his hand.

Even from yards away, March could see the floating glow.

"Extraordinary," Carlotta breathed. She moved closer.

Hamish put a lens over one eye. He stared, one by one, at the stones, holding them up and then dropping them back into a pouch when he was done.

"They're fake," he said.

76

JUST LIKE A THIEF

Hamish shrugged. "These are not the seven magic moonstones," he said. "They are depressingly ordinary."

"Cheaters!" Carlotta screeched.

Blue and Oscar both looked at each other.

"You did it," they said together.

"I don't care who did it," Carlotta said. "The deal is off."

Hamish moved out from the glow of the headlights into the shadows. The pouch swung behind his back.

"You're up, Izzy," March said softly.

She melted into the shadows and inched toward Hamish.

"Now wait a minute," Blue said. "We can still make a deal. Just let me talk to my partner. You want Thailand, Oscar? I'll go. You're punishing me, right?"

"What are you talking about? You're the one who can't be trusted!"

The sound of sirens invaded the soft sounds of the night. Alarmed, March glanced at Jules. This was not part of the plan.

"What's that?" Carlotta asked in surprise. "Police?"

"If you think they're not real, give the stones back," Blue ordered quickly.

"Sure." Hamish flipped the pouch in the air.

The sirens grew louder, and suddenly the trees flashed red.

"Mr. Tarscher, get me out of here!" Carlotta shrieked.

March could see Izzy on the other side of the Hummer. The sirens were getting closer. She could get caught in the headlights if she didn't get out of there. Hamish had already flipped her the moonstones. Why was she still there?

"She froze," Darius said. "Scared. I'll go."

Darius was gone in a moment, sneaking through the bushes toward the car.

Suddenly Carlotta let out a shrill scream. "Where are my BONDS?"

A green Audi shot out onto the road. March had a quick glimpse of Oscar driving.

"OSCAR!" Blue screamed in fury.

Two police cars roared up.

"What should we do?" Jules asked.

"I don't know!" March hissed, panicked. "I've run out of ideas!"

The police got out of the car. A blue Subaru drove up and, with a screech of brakes, slid onto the shoulder. Mike Shannon tumbled out. He held a small camera in front of his face.

"I'm here at the midnight transfer of the moonstones," he intoned. "Desperate heiress Carlotta Grimstone has struck the deal of her life with ruthless criminals —"

"Turn off that camera, you imbecile! Do you know who I am?" Carlotta sneered. She turned to the cop. "Officer, do you know how much I give to the police every year?"

A flashlight swung toward Carlotta, and she threw up her arm to shade her face. "Turn that thing off! Ten million in bonds has been *stolen*! Somebody search somebody!"

"I'm just the chauffeur," Hamish said in a friendly way to a young cop.

"There!" Blue shouted, pointing. "There's the thief!"

The beam of the cop's flashlight landed on a surprised Izzy.

"It's a kid gang!" Blue cried. "That's who you want to question! And there's more of them in the woods!"

In the glow of the lights, a panicked Izzy wound up for a sidewinder pitch. The pouch sailed in the air, above the Hummer, above Carlotta, above the police and Mike Shannon. Like a bridal bouquet with unerring aim for a maid of honor, it landed in March's outstretched hands.

"SCATTER!" Darius shouted. He grabbed Izzy and took off through the woods.

March looked at Jules. They ran.

77

CATAMOUNT LAKE

They cut right through the woods, scratched by branches and tripping over roots. They ran blindly, not remembering exactly where the path had been. Panic had taken over, and they forgot everything in a rush to safety.

They burst out onto a small beach. The lake lapped and gurgled against the shore. The water was black and rippled with the breeze. Distant thunder rumbled. "What now?" Jules asked, panting. "Where are we?"

"I don't know. I'm still trying to figure out what *happened*. I hope Darius and Izzy are okay."

"If I had to bet on anyone getting away, it would be Darius and Izzy."

"At least we have the moonstones," March said. "The real ones."

Jules spun around. "Which way is the town? Where's the trail? Which way should we go?"

March squinted. Off in the distance, there was a dock. A white boat with a red light began to chug away from it. The light began to revolve as the boat picked up speed.

"Police boat," March said.

"Who do you think they're chasing? Oscar?"

"Us."

With the lake at their backs and the police in the woods, they were surrounded. They leaped over the boulders and stumbled onto a narrow trail. They ran, hearing the call of the police over the water. They ran, hoping to intersect to a wider road, a road to town and safety. A light, misty rain began to fall.

Instead, they dead-ended at a cliff.

They looked up at the face of it. The cliff of their nightmares.

"Jules . . ."

"I know."

He put his hand out just to make sure it was real. It was as though he knew every fissure, every bump.

The police boat's searchlight swept the beach they'd stopped on only minutes before.

"Maybe *this* is the way to break the curse," Jules said. "Defy it."

March felt his pocket. The seven moonstones were stuffed inside. He remembered the feeling in the tunnel, how the stones were forcing him to fall.

And now, forcing him to climb. He felt the compulsion take him over.

"Come on," Jules said. Her eyes glittered with a strange, avid light. "There's lots of handholds; I can see them from here." She hauled herself up a few feet.

The moon seemed to yank him upward, calling him. After a few yards March risked a look down. The police boat searchlight was moving clockwise. It would be here soon, spotlighting a boy and a girl on a cliff face at midnight.

Jules was so much higher than he was. March felt dizzy. He paused for a moment. Sweat stung his eyes. He tried to wipe his forehead on his sleeve. His fingers slipped on the wet rock, and a roar of terror ripped through him.

"March . . . you have to go faster," Jules called down to him. "It will all be over in a minute. We can do it."

Why did he feel so . . . heavy? March wished he could wipe away the sweat on his forehead. He leaned his head against his sleeve, trying to wipe it. Then he reached up and found another handhold.

Jules looked down. "Only a few more yards to the top from here! Almost there!"

The boat moved down the shore. March reached for the next handhold and moved his right foot along the ledge above. He found the foothold and pushed off. He pulled himself up to what he saw, with relief, was a narrow ledge. Big enough to balance, just wide enough to even let go with both hands. He didn't have the courage for that, but he let go with one hand to wipe his forehead. If he leaned in against the rock, he felt solid.

But strange. What was this heavy feeling? Fear? Was that why he was finding it so hard to move? He could feel the pouch of stones in his pocket, weighing him down.

Stones in your pocket. You don't want to be hanging over water with stones in your pocket.

"Almost there," Jules called.

She's moving so fast.

She's moving too *fast.*

Alarm suddenly clanged inside March. "Jules!" he called. "Don't . . ."

Time slowed down. The agony of Alfie's fall repeated. Jules's hand, grabbing the next hold, the loose rock coming off, her foot sliding, and then Jules, falling.

78

DON'T LET GO

Time stopped.

He had one chance.

And he saw the two of you, holding hands and falling.

He had all the time in the world.

Here's a C grip. Wrist to wrist. It's a catch grip.

Her arm out, her eyes wide, and he was there, he was! His hand shot out, and, with all his energy, he pressed against the rock, knowing the shock of the catch might send him flying backward into space with her. She made the catch; he had her wrist; she had his wrist; he was still on the rock, hideously unbalanced, but hanging on.

For now.

He didn't have the strength to pull her up. She was in midair, her legs windmilling.

"Stop. Moving." He had to force the words out; he was concentrating so hard on holding her.

She looked up at him, her eyes wide with fear.

"Let go," she said.

"What?"

"If you don't, you'll fall, too." Jules's face was strained with effort. "You'll . . . break the curse. You'll survive."

"Not . . . letting . . . go." March got the words out through gritted teeth. "Remember?"

The police boat was almost at the cliff. The searchlight coming.

His hand was slick with sweat. Sweat pouring down his neck. His hand was going numb.

He saw the reverse curse in a flash in his head.

Fortune's wheel reverses,
Thus fortune's child must bide
Till the night of rare moon rising.
The portal opens, eventide.
Time reverses by your hand.
The captured lights returning,
Fate's wheel stops — then begins anew,
Your fate annulled, your future earning.

He leaned hard against the rock. Straining, he reached the string of the pouch. Grunting with the effort, planting his feet, he withdrew the pouch. With his face against the rock and holding Jules with one hand, he could only get a limited range of motion. With the tips of his fingers, he began to swing the pouch in a circle.

Because suddenly it was all so clear.

Time reverses by your hand . . .

Swing the stones counterclockwise.

The captured lights returning.

Captured moonlight. Let the stones fly into the air. Return the captured moonlight to the sky.

Fate's wheel stops —

The motion of the swing sent the moonstones high over their heads, spilling like a constellation of stars out into the black night air. All seven, beautiful and pure. So bright, they matched the moonlight. They seemed to hang for the longest of moments. . . .

Then begins anew.

And then dropped, all together, clustered in a mass. Disappeared into darkness. Would he hear the splash when they hit the lake?

Instead, a faint tinkle. The searchlight went out.

The moonstones had smashed the light!

The heaviness left his legs and arms. The dread unspooled like a thread. He felt strength and purpose fill his muscles, and he smiled against the rock, tasting grit and sweat. He was here, and Jules was here, and there was not one doubt in his mind that it was now midnight, and they were both thirteen years old.

Your fate annulled, your future earning.

And suddenly it seemed impossibly easy to swing his sister gently forward, bringing her against the rock, and *steady, steady, steady,* hold her until she found a place to rest.

79

FOLLOW THE FALLS

They got to the top and looked down. The police boat looked small from here. It chugged along the shore, but without the searchlight, it would be impossible to spot two small shadows on top of a cliff. Men were moving along the shore, sweeping the brush with flashlights.

March and Jules followed a narrow path. Soon they saw the fissure in the rocks. When they walked inside, the temperature dropped immediately. The ice was thick along the walls, but after their adventure on the cliff, it was a pleasure to walk carefully and slowly, enjoying the cold air.

"Listen," Jules said, and he stopped.

Water flowing, rushing. "The waterfall."

The blue moonlight penetrated even here, illuminating the wall.

"Look," Jules said. "There's a fissure there. At the bottom."

They had to lie flat on the ground to really see it, then chip away at a scrim of ice that covered it, reflecting like a mirror. When March put his eye to the opening, he saw a sandy chamber, and beyond it, the falls.

They were able to lie flat and slither inside. They stood in a tall chamber, hit from the spray of the waterfall. They walked forward, and there it was, now a rushing fall of water over the rocks, spilling into the lake below.

"That night it would have been a torrent," Jules said. "These rocks would have been wet. Maybe there was black ice. And here is where she slipped and went over."

March tried to imagine Alfie at that moment. Watching her body go backward. Did he see her face? Did he see her astonishment, her fear? Sadness invaded him as he thought of Alfie, watching the love of his life fall away.

Alfie had hiked down again, Ham had said, risking his own life and his capture. He'd searched and searched; he had made his way back to their car and to where he and Maggie had been living. He had picked up his children and made the decision to run.

He had protected them by separating them. Whether the plan had been right or wrong, it had worked.

Now standing up here, March understood it all. *Follow the falls to day.* Well, it was night, but had he done everything Alfie had wanted him to?

Alfie, ever practical, would probably say, *Good, you're not dead. But couldn't you manage to keep the moonstones?*

"Was it all real?" March asked. "The moonstones, the curse?"

"We'll never know," Jules said. "I only know what I felt. That I had to climb. That I couldn't hold on anymore. And then I could."

"I felt it, too. And the moonstones hit the searchlight. What are the odds of that?"

"I wouldn't take the bet."

"We lost the fortune."

"Yeah. Stinks."

"And Mike Shannon will want revenge. And Oscar. And Blue."

"Yeah," Jules agreed. "And we have no leverage. No money. No gemstones."

"Things aren't so great."

She grinned. "Couldn't be worse."

"Look," March said. "It's clearing."

The clouds had thinned, and the moon was full and round and luminous. They were high above the lake and could see its full expanse, even glimpse the shadowy outlines of Carlotta's grand mansion.

Had Alfie sat up here as a kid, gazing at a life he couldn't have?

On the other side they could now make out the lights of the town.

"Let's go down," March said.

The trail wound down the gentler side of the mountain. A well-used hiking trail, it was easy to follow, even in the dark.

They hit an overlook halfway down and paused to check their progress. They were close to the town now, to the glowing lights.

Below was a small roadhouse with a blinking, red neon light.

DANO

And, underneath that:

JAZZ AND SPAGHETTI

March felt something rise in him, a bubble of air and laughter.

"Dano!" he cried.

Jules turned to him. "You know that place?"

He shook his head. "No. But Alfie did. His last words — he said, 'Day,' and I said, 'Don't die,' but he was already trying to get out the word, and he said, 'No,' and I thought he was saying to me that he had to die, but he was just *saying the word. Dano.* Follow the falls to *Dano.*"

He pointed. "And there it is."

80

DANO

They walked across a pitted and poorly maintained parking lot jammed with cars. They could hear a guitar and piano playing a funky riff. Pushing open the green door, they were hit with a wave of warmth and light and laughter.

They stood uncertainly in the entrance. Waitstaff in jeans and black T-shirts threaded through the tables, holding trays with plates and glasses high over the heads of diners. The bar to their left was packed with customers, most of whom seemed to be consuming burgers and beers and exchanging jokes with the bartender.

"Do you think normal will ever feel normal again?" March asked.

Jules grinned. "Look at who you're talking to. What's normal?"

March grinned back. "Turn left, every time."

A smiling woman with red curly hair walked forward. "Good evening. You two looking for your parents?"

The question stymied them.

There were no parents to look for. Not anymore.

Just an innocent question could open up a whole cavern of empty. They would have it every day of their lives.

"No," March said. "We . . ."

He stopped. A woman customer stood at the coat check, a tiny room with a half door. She handed the girl a playing card ripped in half. The girl handed her a raincoat. The woman put a dollar in the jar and joined her companions and walked out into the night.

March dug into his pocket and took out the ripped joker. He swallowed. "I need to pick something up. For my dad."

The red-haired woman took the card. "I'll take this to Sarah for you." Then she looked at the card more closely. There was just a beat, enough to put March's nerves on alert. But she handed the card to the girl at the coat check, said a few words, smiled briefly at March and Jules, and moved off.

"Should we go?" Jules muttered. "I don't like this. Did you see how she hesitated?"

"I don't know."

A meaty hand descended on his shoulder from behind. "Can I help you?"

March turned and found himself looking at a hard stare. The guy was tall and built, and his manner was polite, but March wouldn't call it welcoming.

"I came to pick something up," March said.

"You need the other half of the card." The man shrugged. "That's the way it works."

"Since when?"

His smile was hard. "Since now."

Jules stepped forward. She held out the other half.

The man raised an eyebrow. He took the card, walked to the window, with March and Jules trailing behind. He held out a hand, and the girl in the coat check — who March now realized strongly resembled the older woman with the red curls — handed him the other half. He placed the two halves together carefully.

Then he turned and grinned, and was transformed into a friendly human.

"I'm Joey Dano," he said. "And you are . . ."

"March and Jules McQuin," March said.

"I thought so. Even though I haven't seen you since you were knee-high. How's your dad?"

"Not so good," March said. "He's dead."

Joey Dano's face crumpled. Tears sprang to his eyes. "No."

"About a month ago, in Amsterdam. He fell off a roof."

"Oh . . ." Joey Dano wiped his eyes. "We grew up together. Did he tell you? No? Alfie would keep that close, I guess. Never wanted to get me in trouble. Liked my burgers, though." Tears were now running down his face. "Oh man, I'm sorry, kids. Loved your dad, that's all. Let me get you what he left with me. 'Joey,' he said that night, 'Keep this for me, will you? For as long as it takes?' God, he was a sight. I cleaned him up, gave him a place to just be quiet, our private dining room, all to himself, gave him food he didn't eat. I offered him a car, a steak, a bed to sleep in. . . . 'No,' he said. 'I gotta get to my kids; I just need you to keep this.' So I gave him the card, a fresh deck, and he ripped it in half, and then he said — and I'll never forget it — 'I might not be the one who comes, so it's gotta be both halves, you understand?' I've never moved anything, never looked; what Alfie said was good enough for me. Whatever it is, I kept it, and now it's yours."

All the while he was talking, Joey Dano was moving, going into the coat check, mopping his tears with a handkerchief, and crying again. He handed them a small nylon duffel, light and small enough to carry easily. A getaway pack.

"Thank you," March said. "But we have to go now."

"You'll come back? I'll feed you, tell you some stories?"

"You bet," Jules said.

"That's a promise?"

"It's a promise."

They walked out with the duffel. The door shut behind them, and it was quiet again. March hitched the duffel on his shoulder. They walked halfway down the road in the direction of the middle school.

"We've got to look," Jules said. "I can't stand it."

"Those trees up there — the pine trees. We'll stop there."

They walked into the shade of a massive tree, ducking under the lowest branch. It was pitch-dark here, a green dark that smelled fresh and piney.

March unzipped the duffel.

Inside were a pair of socks, a pair of briefs, and a T-shirt. A toothbrush and toothpaste. A soap dish. A razor. The old-fashioned kind, with the straight-edge razor you lift out and replace. It was just a getaway pack.

"Nothing," Jules said.

March opened the soap dish. Inside was a bar of soap. No design or name carved in the soap, just a smooth, perfect oval.

"When I was a kid," March murmured, "Alfie used to carve ducks out of hotel soap."

"Charming," Jules said. "So?"

"He was good with a razor blade."

He reached for the razor, removed the blade, and gripped it. He began to carefully scrape away at the soap. Within a minute or so he felt it hit something. He scraped deeper, then used his fingers to peel away the crumbling soap. The scent of soap mingled with pine.

He brushed the soap splinters away. He held the stone up to catch the faint ray of moonlight that had penetrated the thick green leaves.

The Makepeace Diamond picked up the light and sent it dancing.

EPILOGUE

Juggling paper bags, March slid the key into the lock.

He walked into the apartment and tossed the bags on the table. "Dinner!"

"It's about time. I'm starving," Jules said. She leaped off the trapeze they'd hung in the living room.

"I'll set the table," Izzy called from the cushions of the deep sofa. There were four sofas in the living room. They'd soon learned that for movie watching on the flat screen, they each wanted their own space.

She accidentally bumped into Darius, who was standing looking out at the river.

"Just checking up on my yacht," he said. "Next week, Bermuda."

A jumble of bikes was tangled up near the front door. A long table ran the length of the room, strewn with Izzy's motherboards, Jules's drawings, Darius's manga, March's books.

There was an entire cabinet devoted to snacks.

It was surprisingly easy to live on your own. Especially when you buy a whole building.

The other apartments were now used as game rooms, media rooms, and one had been turned into a swimming pool and spa. One was a small gym with a climbing wall (March avoided that one). There was a garden on the roof, and a gardener to take care of it.

That night went down in criminal history as the crime

of the *new* century. Seven magic moonstones had disappeared, along with ten million in bonds. Oscar Ford had vanished.

Blue was cleared of suspicion, but not before becoming a media star. Shortly afterward, she founded her own production company, thanks to a mysterious investor. "Particle Zoo" was a hit on alternative radio stations. She was in talks to develop her own reality TV show.

Mike Shannon was doing camera commercials in Japan. Making a nice living. March had offered a production company a hefty budget to produce them. They'd never go on the air. But Shannon didn't know that. It was enough to know that Shannon was out of their hair for a good long time.

Hamish had been happy to help them with details of the building purchase, just for the chance to fence the Makepeace Diamond. Now they were even. It was a good start to the next phase of the relationship.

Darius pushed a stack of files and two laptops to the end of the table. He tossed napkins and forks down. Izzy brought plates and a big spoon for the guacamole. Jules handed him a burrito.

"Saw Blue on YouTube today," Darius said. "She's up to three million hits."

"She's getting famous," Izzy agreed.

"Just the way she wanted," Jules said.

The ironic twist to her smile reminded March of Alfie. He missed his father, sometimes so fiercely he wanted to howl, but it helped to have Jules. With a lift of her eyebrow or a sudden smile, he caught a glimpse of his dad every day.

Now when he felt something was missing, he could just look across the room, and there she was.

March pushed aside the file marked POSSIBLE JOBS. He glanced at the thickest file of all: GETTING BACK AT BLUE.

"We have all kinds of time," he said. "If you're going to do it . . ."

"Don't do it stupid!" they all chorused.

March took a big bite of burrito. Spicy. Just the way he and Alfie liked it.

As Alfie would say:

Living sure is easy when you have twenty million in the bank.